D1623957

BAMBOO KINGDOM

THE DARK SUN

BAMBOO KINGDOM

BAMBOO KINGDOM

THE DARK SUN

ERIN HUNTER

HARPER
An Imprint of HarperCollinsPublishers

Special thanks to Rosie Best

Bamboo Kingdom #4: The Dark Sun
Copyright © 2023 Working Partners Ltd.
All rights reserved. Printed in the United States of America.
No part of this book may be used or reproduced in any manner whatsoever without written
permission except in the case of brief quotations embodied in critical articles and reviews. For
information address HarperCollins Children's Books, a division of HarperCollins Publishers, 195
Broadway, New York, NY 10007.
www.harpercollinschildrens.com

Library of Congress Control Number: 2023933385
ISBN 978-0-06-302211-9

Typography by Corina Lupp
23 24 25 26 27 LBC 5 4 3 2 1

First Edition

Special thanks to CCPPG for their inspiration and creativity, and for enabling Erin Hunter to bring Bamboo Kingdom to the world.

DRAGON MOUNTAIN

THE NORTHERN FOREST

FEAST CLEARING

THE SOUTHERN FOREST

*One moon has passed since Leaf, Ghost, and Rain became
the new Dragon Speakers of the Bamboo Kingdom.*

PROLOGUE

CROOKEDCLAW SAT ON THE sloping trunk of a tree, leaning against the splintered stump of one of the branches, watching the vast troop gather around the crack in the earth. This was the dark place at the heart of the Broken Forest, where the rocks were black and strange, and wisps of steam still occasionally rose from the caverns far below. Whatever long-ago event had split the earth, it had also crumbled rock columns into heaps of stone and blown over most of the trees, so that even the ones that had survived now grew at odd angles.

Brawnshanks, leader of the golden monkeys, had called his troop to gather in this place, and they had come—more than three hundred of them, by Crookedclaw's reckoning, swarming along the ground and swinging over the leaning trees.

She knew them all. Nothing went on in the Broken Forest

that escaped Crookedclaw's keen eye. She knew which bands were strong, bonded families, and which were fractious groups of monkeys who would throw each other into the crevice for a single cherry. She knew which monkeys had long-running feuds, which had mated against their bands' wishes. In any troop, there were always twice as many petty dramas and disagreements as there were monkeys, and Crookedclaw knew them all.

Brawnshanks sat beside the crevice in the ground, watching with satisfaction as his troop assembled around him. Golden monkeys from all over the Bamboo Kingdom had come to join him in the last few months, hearing of brave, clever Brawnshanks and his secret plan to put the kingdom back into the paws of the monkeys. And Crookedclaw suspected they were about to find out just what their leader was planning.

A ripple of excitement ran through the assembled monkeys, hoots and jeers rising as the Strong Arms pushed their way through the bands, elbowing and puffing out their chests. They were led by Silvermane, the head of the Strong Arms, with her lieutenants following behind her. Jitterpaws still walked with one arm dangling, useless, after it had been broken in the fight with the white panda.

Between them, something was staggering along, prodded every few steps with a stick to keep it moving. As they pushed through to the open space where Brawnshanks sat, the Strong Arms parted to reveal their prisoner: a pangolin. She shuffled forward on her back legs, the claws of her front paws clasped nervously in front of her chest. Crookedclaw nodded to herself. The Strong Arms had done their thuggish job well. The pangolin was terrified.

"Welcome," said Brawnshanks, with an expansive gesture. "Thank you for coming. May I know your name?"

The pangolin looked confused. Of course she did—Crookedclaw knew she hadn't come here willingly.

"C-curling Star," said the pangolin.

"What a lovely name," said Brawnshanks. In the tree next to Crookedclaw, a band of monkeys sniggered to each other, and Curling Star looked up, her beady eyes scanning the tree branches. Crookedclaw shot the band a fierce look, and they fell silent.

Brawnshanks went on, still speaking in a soft, reassuring tone. "I asked you to come because I know that the pangolins know more about the Great Dragon than any creature—apart from the Dragon Speakers, of course—and I need to ask you some questions. Come, sit near me."

Curling Star hesitated, but eventually took a few steps toward Brawnshanks and sat down.

"Tell me, Curling Star," said Brawnshanks. "How was the Great Dragon created?"

Curling Star let out a soft gasp, then hesitated. "I don't know," she said. "I—I thought the Great Dragon always existed. But . . . but . . . even if I did know the story, I wouldn't tell you!" she gabbled, and then curled up into a ball with a frightened squeak.

"Why on earth not?" said Brawnshanks, putting his face close to the pangolin's armored surface.

The pangolin didn't uncurl, so her reply was muffled, her head completely covered by her scaly tail. "You—you'll do something bad with it!" she yelped.

Crookedclaw slipped down the sloping tree and walked up behind the curled pangolin. She bent down to whisper between the interlocking scales.

"You know more than you're saying," she said, and Curling Star jumped, uncurling slightly in her surprise. Crookedclaw stamped her paw down on the pangolin's tail, so she couldn't completely re-curl. "And you will tell us what you know, or the other pangolins we're watching will suffer for it."

The pangolin yelped. Crookedclaw smirked. These creatures were so gullible. Curling Star was the first pangolin they had caught, but it seemed she completely believed Crookedclaw's bluff.

"All right," the pangolin squeaked. "All right, I'll tell you the story." She cleared her throat nervously and scratched at the ashy rock. "Well, long ago, there wasn't one dragon—there were two. The Light Dragon who ruled over the day, and fire, and the truth, and things like that. And the Dark Dragon who ruled over the night and shadows and stories and caves, and suchlike. But one day . . . a m-monkey brought them together."

"How?" Brawnshanks demanded, slapping his hands down on the rock in front of Curling Star's nose. She recoiled, and tried to curl up again, but Crookedclaw was too fast for her and pressed down on her back so she couldn't move.

"I don't know!" Curling Star gasped. "I swear on the Dragon, nobody knows except for—"

She broke off with a tiny, angry growl, and put her claws over her eyes.

We have her, Crookedclaw thought, giving Brawnshanks a sly nod.

"Go," she said, turning to Silvermane. "And pull scales off those other pangolins until Curling Star tells us *who* knows how the monkey did it."

Silvermane chuckled, nodded, and started to walk off in a random direction.

"No, please, it's the Children," Curling Star spluttered. "All right? It's the Children of the Dragon, they're the ones that know."

"And who *are* these Children of the Dragon?" Brawnshanks asked, scratching his chin.

"They . . . they're an order of pangolins," said Curling Star, in a small voice. "They're descended from the pangolins who were there, when the Great Dragon was created. But they keep their secrets to themselves. They don't speak much, and when they do, it's all in riddles. They don't even tell their secrets to other pangolins. You can pull *my* scales off," she added, raising her head in shaky defiance. "There's nothing more I can tell you."

"These Children of the Dragon *will* tell us their secrets," Crookedclaw told Brawnshanks.

"Whatever you're up to, the new Dragon Speakers will stop you!" Curling Star said.

Brawnshanks chortled. "Three panda cubs, who've been Dragon Speakers for a month? They think they're strong, because they defeated the fool Dusk, but they'll learn their place if they try to cross me."

Crookedclaw shoved Curling Star into the arms of Silvermane. "Take her away," she said. "Keep her under guard. She may be useful again."

The pangolin protested and cried out as the Strong Arms dragged her away, but Crookedclaw wasn't listening. Brawnshanks had risen and was climbing to the top of the closest broken tree, high above the gathered monkeys. He gestured to her to follow, and Crookedclaw did, using the splintered wood for her paw holds. Brawnshanks stopped where the tree had bent and then broken in two, at the peak of what was now a giant arch of blackened wood.

"Good work, Crookedclaw," he said. "I will need your skills more than ever before, if we are to succeed."

"We will," said Crookedclaw.

"And once we have the pangolins' secrets," Brawnshanks went on, his eyes glinting as he looked out over his enormous troop, the greatest fighting force the Bamboo Kingdom had ever seen, "then every last leaf and stone of this kingdom will be mine."

CHAPTER ONE

LEAF SAT IN THE branches of a tall gingko tree, looking out
over the lush bamboo-filled Southern Forest. She held the
green Dragon Speaker stone tucked in her paw, next to her
white grip pad, and listened to the wind in the leaves. She
watched the round black-and-white shapes of her fellow
pandas—some lounging in patches of sunlight, some climbing trees, many collecting bamboo for the Feast of High Sun.
A few walked the panda path, the flattened grass trail that
wound its way down the side of one steep hill and up the next.
The river glittered through the trees to her right, and to her
left lay the flat-topped feast clearing hill. Beyond it, the sharp
rock columns and steep, forested slopes rolled on until they
were lost in pale mist.

Leaf saw Rain down below, sitting with a group of smaller

creatures, mostly mice and flying squirrels, gathered around her. She couldn't hear them, but she could tell that they were asking for Rain's advice about something. Rain nodded as she listened, and then held up her blue stone. It caught the light and glinted for a moment.

It was just like Rain to call to the Great Dragon then and there. She always wanted to answer creatures' questions as soon as possible, even if that meant disappointing them if the Dragon had no advice to share. It was sort of admirable.

Or it would be, Leaf thought, *if she was only doing it to be helpful, and not so she can spend more time napping and splashing in the river.*

Leaf preferred to get petitioners to wait a while, so that if the Dragon didn't have anything to say she could at least give their problem some thought. And Ghost . . . well, he was trying to adjust to life away from the mountains and his leopard upbringing, but his advice still seemed to work for plenty of creatures.

She felt an odd burst of pride as she spotted him too, his pure white fur standing out among the throng of ordinary pandas. He was walking and talking seriously with the old panda Mist.

She could hardly believe that she'd only known the two of them for a bit more than a month. They were so different, but she knew that if she ever needed help, they would be there. Each of them had been tasked with the care of a different part of the kingdom—Rain the river and the moon, Ghost the mountains and the stars, and Leaf the trees and the sun.

They were still working out just what that meant, but every time one of them felt something new and ran to the others to share it, she felt the euphoria of that first meeting in the snow all over again. She loved them as dearly as if they'd grown up together as cubs. Possibly even more so.

A rustling and cracking of leaves and a flurry of movement down below caught Leaf's attention, and she leaned over to see what was going on.

"Dragon Speaker Rain, a word?" some panda cried, loud enough for their voice to carry up into the branches of Leaf's tree. She sighed as she saw the pandas who had stomped into the clearing, scattering the small creatures who'd gathered around Rain. It was Azalea and Granite, looking annoyed, and trailing reluctantly behind them were Blossom and Ginseng.

Leaf slipped off her perch and down the trunk of the tree, moving in more of a controlled tumble than a climb. She landed on her behind and rolled to her paws to hurry to the clearing.

It had been a shock when Blossom and Ginseng had returned to the Prosperhill a few days ago. Rain, Leaf, and Ghost had prepared themselves for a fight as soon as they'd seen them trudging up the panda path, remembering their faces snarling down from the side of the Dragon Mountain, goaded to attack the Dragon Speakers by the impostor Dusk Deepwood. All three siblings still bore the scars from that fight. And for Rain and Ghost it was worse, because they'd had to live with Blossom and Ginseng under Dusk's reign, enduring their bullying and their lies.

But perhaps the most shocking thing about Blossom and Ginseng's return to the Prosperhill had been that they weren't looking for a fight.

Leaf made it to the clearing just as Rain was facing off with Ginseng—at least, *Rain* was facing off. Ginseng was standing back, a worried look on his face. Leaf didn't blame him. Rain looked furious, as if she might be about to do something very un-Speaker-like.

"I'll take care of this one," Leaf panted, running up beside her sister. "You were busy with the squirrels, right?"

"Yes," Rain snarled. "Before these four scared half of them off."

"Well, why don't you go and find them?" Leaf said. *Come on,* she willed her sister. *You know you can't be impartial about these two. Just let me handle it.*

Rain looked at her, and sighed. "Fine, I will. Granite, tell Leaf what you told me." She turned and stomped away, casting angry glances back at Blossom and Ginseng.

"Leaf," Granite said, "these two are causing trouble again. They've taken much more than their share of the bamboo; they're guarding that good patch over in the shade of the big rock column like it belongs to them!"

"We can sit and eat where we want," Granite grumbled. "That bamboo doesn't belong to you, either!"

"Last time I looked, we were still living together, and that means we should be sharing everything," Azalea put in, with a sharp sneer. Leaf tried to hide her sigh.

Not this again.

Some of the pandas wanted to split up now and find their own territories, to live the way pandas had before the Great Flood had driven so many creatures from their old homes. But others wanted to stick together, the same way they'd lived ever since. Azalea was one of the keenest to leave, although Leaf noted she hadn't actually left—she just liked to complain about it.

"In the old days that would have been *our* bamboo," Blossom grumbled. "If we weren't all living crammed into this territory together, there wouldn't be a problem here."

"But we *are* living together," said Leaf, trying to be as patient as she could. "You two chose to come back here, and we all gave you that second chance—but you have to realize that means sharing with the others."

"We know," Ginseng said. Blossom threw him a slightly grumpy look, but then she sighed and nodded.

"Yes, we know. Sorry," she said. "We're just not used to living like this anymore. Sorry, Azalea."

Leaf blinked, pleased but surprised. Rain had told her what Blossom had been like even before Dusk came to the Prosperhill, so she hadn't expected getting an apology out of her to be this easy.

They really are trying, she thought.

Azalea didn't look entirely convinced.

"Why don't you two go and fetch those tender young stems from that patch?" Leaf said. "We can share them around at the next feast."

"That's fair," said Ginseng. "Come on." He nudged Blossom and the two of them left the clearing.

"I still don't trust them," Azalea said quietly.

"I know, but we have to give them a chance," Leaf said. "They're a bit selfish, but if they want to make things right, we should let them."

Azalea just shook her head and stomped off, with Granite on her heels.

It was almost time for the Feast of High Sun. Leaf was gathering her own mouthful of bamboo stems for the feast when there was a rustling on the other side of the patch. She looked up to see Pebble breaking through, his jaws full of thick bamboo. He dropped it and sat down.

"Hello, Leaf," he said.

"Hello," she said. She clamped her teeth down on a bamboo cane and snapped it off with a satisfying cracking sound.

Pebble sat and watched her.

She sighed as she added the cane to the pile between her paws. "How are you doing, Pebble?" she asked.

"Oh, fine," said Pebble. He rolled one of his bamboo canes under his front paw. "I mean . . . I'm fine. It's just . . ."

It's Rain, Leaf thought.

"It's Rain," said Pebble.

Leaf nodded sympathetically. "She *still* won't talk to you?"

"It's not that she *won't* talk to me," Pebble said, flopping down to sit beside the bamboo. "It's just that she . . . she *doesn't.* She'll answer if I ask her a question or speak to her directly, but she never talks to me first, and it's just not the same. I've told her I'm sorry, and she said she understood, but . . . what if we can never be friends again? What if I've let her down so badly that I've ruined our friendship forever?"

Leaf sighed. In a lot of ways, she could hardly blame Rain for holding a grudge against the panda who'd been her best friend, when he had sided with Dusk and the others. He hadn't helped Rain when she and her adopted mother Peony had been trapped in a pit by Dusk and the monkeys. He'd even turned her in to Dusk when she tried to escape. He said it had all happened in a flash of confusion and panic, but if Dasher had done something like that, Leaf wasn't sure she'd forgive him easily, either.

"Rain just needs time," she told Pebble. "It's obvious that you're truly sorry. I'm sure she'll come around, but you can't rush her."

"I know," Pebble said. He picked a leaf off the bamboo cane and crushed it in his grip pad. "It's just . . . the longer I wait . . ." He let out a heavy sigh. "She's just always hanging around with Lychee. . . ."

"Well, perhaps he's her best friend right now," Leaf said. "But there's no rule that a panda can't have more than one best friend!"

Pebble shifted his paws. "But what if she wants him to be more than that? And I thought . . . well, I wanted . . ."

Oh! Leaf felt her fur prickle with embarrassment. *So that's the problem.* Leaf had never given much thought to finding a mate for herself, but of course Rain and Pebble might have started to have feelings for each other!

Now that she understood, Leaf's heart ached for Pebble. He was right—Rain was spending a *lot* of time with Lychee, the young panda who had found his way to the Prosperhill after the Dragon Speakers had taken their place there. It made perfect sense to Leaf that Rain would seek out the company of the one young male in the forest who *wasn't* involved in Dusk's plotting, who never rejected her like the others did. But she could see the pain of it on Pebble's face.

"Did you ever tell her how you felt?" she asked Pebble.

Pebble shook his head.

"Well . . . If she feels the same, then she'll come around with time, I'm sure of it," Leaf said. "And if she doesn't, then you should be glad that she's found someone who makes her happy, right?"

"It sounds very easy when you put it like that."

As Leaf tried to think of something reassuring to say, she found herself staring into the waving bamboo . . . and she saw something moving through it. A flash of red, a ruffle of gold. Leaf gasped, and her heart thumped in her chest.

The Great Dragon!

She would never stop feeling the thrill in her bones when

the Dragon came to her like this. She clutched the green stone
to her chest, and then glanced at Pebble.

"It's the Dragon," she said, giving him an apologetic smile.

"Go, go," said Pebble, waving one paw. "I'll carry your bamboo up to the feast clearing."

"Thanks, Pebble!" Leaf said. She tracked the movement of
the waving bamboo, and her eyes were drawn to a tall ginkgo
tree nearby. She padded over to it and began to climb, digging
her strong claws into the bark to lift herself up to the first low
branch.

What does the Dragon want to tell me? she wondered, her heart
pounding as she pressed up onto the next branch, and then
the next, higher and higher. *Something about the trees? Or is it the
sun?*

The golden leaves of the ginkgo ruffled around her, flick-
ers of red occasionally passing behind them, as she clambered
all the way up to the highest branch that would support her
weight. She held on to the trunk as she looked out over the
Bamboo Kingdom, but she didn't feel afraid even as the tree
swayed in the breeze.

With one paw on the trunk, Leaf held the green Speaker
stone close to her heart, fixed her eyes on the wide blue sky,
and waited, listening.

The Dragon's voice always came to her as a gust of warm
wind at first, and sure enough, a soft roar spiraled around her
perch on the tree and filled her ears. The words came second. The Dragon's voice echoed, just as it had in the chamber

inside the distant mountain.

"*Leaf*," said the Dragon, and Leaf gave a small, happy shudder. The voice was deep and musical, and just hearing it always made Leaf feel as if wherever she was, she was at home.

"I'm here," she whispered back.

"*Heed my warning*," said the Dragon. "*A Dark Sun will rise*."

Leaf shuddered again, but not so happily this time. She looked up at the sun, feeling its warmth on her face as she squinted toward it. It appeared perfectly normal.

A Dark Sun . . . ?

The Dragon was already leaving her; she could feel the air turning colder. She hurried back down the tree, the voice echoing in her head as she dangled from the branches and let herself slip down the side of the trunk. She had to find the others.

The pandas were already gathered in the feast clearing for the Feast of High Sun, so Leaf could make her way quickly to where Rain and Ghost were sitting in the grass.

"The Dragon spoke to me," she said breathlessly, and her siblings looked up with awe in their eyes. They had both heard its voice over the past month, too—Rain in the river, and Ghost under the starlight—but it was still exciting.

"What did it say?" Ghost asked.

"It told me *A Dark Sun will rise*," Leaf said.

Rain blinked at her. "What in the kingdom does that mean? 'A dark sun'?" She thought for a moment, looking up at the sun in the sky just as Leaf had. "Could it mean the moon?"

"The moon rises almost every night," Ghost pointed out. "It must be something else. It sounds ominous to me."

Rain nudged him with one paw. "Leaf can handle it, though," she said. "After all, the sun's your area, right? So the Dragon must know you can do . . . whatever it wants you to do."

Leaf nodded uncertainly as Mist and the other older pandas began to call the pandas to the Feast of High Sun. She recited the blessing along with the rest, the words flowing easily as her mind wandered.

"Great Dragon, at the Feast of High Sun, your humble pandas bow before you. Thank you for the gift of the bamboo, and the peace you bestow upon us."

But she didn't feel very peaceful.

Dusk is defeated, and the kingdom is recovering from the Great Flood, she thought. *So why do I feel like the Dark Sun might mean terrible trouble for all of us?*

CHAPTER TWO

"Get out, you little worm!"

Ghost's ears pricked up as he heard growling and muttering from around the bend of the panda path, a short while after the Feast of Sun Fall that same day. Sounds of cracking bamboo followed, and some panda falling with a heavy *oof!* Ghost frowned and broke into a run up to the top of the hill. He found himself looking up at a tall, twisting pine tree, under which a large area had been flattened into what looked like a big, comfortable nest for a panda. Two pandas were standing over it, glaring down at a smaller one who had apparently used some of the leaves and branches to make his own nest inside theirs.

Ghost's heart sank to see Blossom and Ginseng, and then it sank even more as he realized the young panda lying in the nest with an innocent expression was Pepper.

Just for a moment, he almost wanted to turn and walk away.

No! You're a Dragon Speaker now, he reminded himself. *You have to deal with this.*

Blossom, Ginseng, Ghost, and Pepper had a history that was . . . complicated. Dusk had once thought Pepper was one of the triplets, and Blossom and Ginseng had chased him across the mountainside for that reason. Was Pepper afraid, remembering that chase?

It's Pepper, Ghost thought, *there's no telling what he's thinking.*

After all, Ghost had worked for Dusk too, once, and the cub had never seemed to hold it against him. Now Pepper was looking at Blossom with the same naïve, dreamy expression he always had.

"Look at this." Blossom sniffed at a pile of dislodged leaves. "You've broken the branches and scattered half our bedding!"

"Oh, yes," Pepper said. "I didn't think you'd mind."

Ghost could never tell when Pepper was telling the truth, or one of his extravagantly confident lies.

"*Mind?*" Ginseng snapped. "You've—you've made a nest *in* our nest!"

Ghost hurried toward them, and Blossom looked around as he approached and gave him an aggrieved glare.

"Just in time, *Speaker,*" she said, with just a hint of sarcasm. "You can tell this cub to get out of my nest before I do something I'll regret."

"Pepper, leave these two alone," Ghost said. "Come with

me and we'll find you a much better spot."

"But we don't have our own territory," said Pepper, still looking innocently confused. "So they're supposed to share, aren't they? So I can sleep where I like!"

Ghost dug his claws into the soft earth for a moment. He was tempted to just pick Pepper up by the scruff of his neck, like his adopted mother, Winter, would have done if his litter-mates Shiver, Frost, or Snowstorm had been laying somewhere they shouldn't.

But I have to stop thinking like a snow leopard, he told himself.

"We're all too cramped here as it is," Blossom snarled. "I'm not sharing my sleeping place with this little monster. Go on, get out!"

"What's happening now?" said a voice, and Ghost looked up to see Azalea peering down at him from the rocks higher up the slope.

"Come *on,* Pepper," Ghost muttered urgently. "It may not be against the rules to take someone else's nest, as such, but it—it's not *polite,* is it?"

"We wouldn't have to rely on politeness if we had our own territory," muttered Blossom.

"Why did you come back then?" said another voice, and Ghost turned, his heart sinking, to see a group of pandas converging on the nest. Mist was the one who had spoken, but there were six other pandas with her. Behind them all, with a concerned frown creasing her fur, came Leaf.

"Yeah! If you don't like living together, you should go,"

squeaked little Fir. But Ghost caught Cypress and Horizon giving each other uncomfortable looks. Maybe Fir's parents didn't feel quite the same as their cub?

"Things would be much simpler if we had our own territory," said Azalea. "I hate to agree with Ginseng and Blossom, but they're not wrong."

"But then we wouldn't be with the Dragon Speakers," said Crag.

"We didn't even have a Speaker for a year after the flood, and we did all right," Cypress put in.

"What do you think, Squall?" asked Lily, turning to the elder panda.

Squall sighed. "Pandas are made to live on their own territory," he said. "That's how it's always been. But I'm too old to change my ways again. I will be Squall Prosperhill until the end of my days."

"If the Dragon made us to live alone, then let's just go," said Ginseng, casting a glance at Ghost and then at Leaf, as if waiting for them to contradict him. Ghost looked to Leaf too. Leaf said nothing—her brow just furrowed deeper with worry.

I don't know! he thought, a little desperately. *I've only known I am a panda for a few moons. I don't know what the Dragon wants us to be like!*

Snow leopards lived alone, unless they had cubs to look after. But that was because they needed the territory to hunt, and to avoid too many fights.

But panda food doesn't move, and pandas don't fight—at least, not like leopards do.

"If there was trouble, we'd have to walk a long way to find help," said Crag.

"There wouldn't be trouble if we didn't have trouble-makers," said Azalea, in a muttered tone that sounded like someone who wanted to pretend they were whispering but actually be heard by everybody.

"Like Pepper?" Blossom snapped. She raised a paw, and Ghost tensed, as did half the other pandas. But she didn't hurt Pepper—she just pressed her paw to his back and rolled him unceremoniously out of the nest.

"Hey!" said another voice, and Goji, Pepper's mother, came running down the slope to gather Pepper to her. "You keep your paws off my cub!"

"I wouldn't have to touch your cub if he'd stay away from my nest," Blossom snarled. "Why doesn't he share your nest, if he can't find his own?"

"That's rich coming from a pair of traitors," spat Lily.

"Lily, *don't*," said Crag. "We said we'd let it go."

"*We* didn't say anything, Crag! I'll say what I want about these thugs!" said Lily, and all of a sudden all the pandas seemed to be talking at once, and Ghost realized to his horror that Blossom and Lily were squaring up as if they might actually start swiping at each other.

I was right, pandas don't *fight like leopards—they fight like pandas, which might be worse*, Ghost thought.

"Stop it!" he barked, trying to step between Lily and Blossom. The two pandas didn't push past him to keep fighting, but they glared over his shoulders, and behind them the argument was raging on—Crag calling for Lily to leave it alone, Goji defending Pepper at the top of her voice.

Ghost tried to block out the noise and focus.

He missed the White Spine Mountains. That was somehow the worst thing about all of this—if the pandas could only agree that splitting up was the right thing to do, he would have gone back there without complaint. It was a harder life, food was scarce and the weather was cold and wet, but part of him missed it every time he sat under the stars and looked down at the white stone. Hadn't he been made the Speaker for the mountains? It nagged at him that the Prosperhill pandas had three Dragon Speakers at their paws, but the creatures who lived high in the mountains had none. . . .

Leaving, though, would mean leaving Leaf and Rain. He'd only just met them, and they seemed to want to keep the Prosperhill together, so that was what he would do. He might be the color of snow, but he belonged with them.

"Dragon Speakers," said Squall, "what should we do?"

"Can you ask the Dragon?" Fir suggested.

Ghost noticed that most of the pandas were looking to Leaf, rather than him, and he couldn't really blame them. He was looking to her himself, even though she looked just as lost as he felt.

"I think we should find Rain," he said to her quietly.

"Ghost's right," said Leaf. "We'll go and find Rain, and then . . ." She seemed to cast around for what might happen next. "Then we'll be back," she said eventually.

She tumbled down the rocks to Ghost, and they set off together down the panda path.

They didn't need to discuss where they were going to look for Rain—Ghost instinctively headed downhill toward the river.

"What do we do?" Ghost asked Leaf, once they were out of earshot of the other pandas.

"I . . . honestly don't know," Leaf replied.

Ghost's paws felt heavy as they came to the end of the panda path and climbed down over the rocks to the mossy riverbank. The water had been retreating for a moon or two now, the river slowly ebbing back to its original size after a year of being flooded. From Ghost's perspective, the great expanse of water now looked merely *huge and scary* instead of *absolutely gigantic and terrifying.* A couple of bear-lengths from the edge of the water, the ground took on a strange look— being underwater for a year had covered the rocks in algae and moss, and filled in the gaps with mud. It was no longer as slippery as it had been, but Ghost still trod carefully as he made his way toward the water.

Sure enough, two pandas were out in the river, giggling and splashing. Rain and her new friend, Lychee, were playing with a big floating log, diving under it and then rolling over it in a sort of chase, though Ghost wasn't sure who was chasing who.

Beside him, Leaf gave a heavy sigh. Then she stepped forward and shouted over the rushing of the river.

"Rain! Come out, we need to talk to you!"

Rain bobbed in the water, waving her paws. Then she swam for the shore, with Lychee behind her. Her short, strong paddling motions meant she was at the rocks in a matter of moments, and Lychee almost kept pace with his overlarge paws pushing through the water. His paws made Ghost think that when he had finally finished growing he would be one of the largest bears in the kingdom.

"What's going on?" she asked.

"Dragon Speaker business," said Leaf, with a pointed look over Rain's back at Lychee, as he climbed out of the water.

Rain turned and rocked her body so that her shoulder nudged against his. "Go on, I'll meet you at the feast clearing," she said.

"Okay," said Lychee. Ghost quite liked Lychee—there was a keen perceptiveness in his eyes, and he never seemed to put a paw wrong with Rain. "See you all up there." He padded past the siblings and away into the trees without another word, and Rain climbed up the rocks to sit beside Leaf.

"What's going on?" she asked.

"I know the Dragon put you in charge of the river, but I don't think it meant you to spend all day every day swimming in it," Leaf said. Her tone was light, and she was obviously joking, but Ghost sensed the frustration underneath. Rain clearly did too. She shook herself, sending droplets flying everywhere, and frowned at Leaf.

"That's not fair," she said. "I do my share of work! Anyway, at least creatures always know where to find me. Do I get at you for spending all your time in trees?"

Leaf gave a frustrated sigh. "When I'm in the trees, I'm *watching*—look, that's not important right now," she said.

"She's watching, except when she's napping," Rain muttered to Ghost, and Ghost found himself snorting with laughter.

Leaf glared at both of them. "This is important," she said. "Things are not good in the Prosperhill. You were there, Ghost, you tell her."

Ghost sighed, the laughter leaving him as he remembered the argument. He recounted it to Rain, whose face fell as she listened.

"What can we do?" she asked. "Can we—*should* we—keep everyone here if they don't want to stay?"

"I think we need to talk it through at the next feast, with everyone," Leaf said.

"It sounds like there's a good chance it'll just be a huge argument," said Rain.

"Well, that's true," Leaf said. "But we can't just decide for them, can we?"

"I sort of wish we could," Rain muttered. "But no. That's not what Dragon Speakers are for. That's the sort of thing Dusk would do."

"We could vote," Ghost said quietly. His sisters both turned to look at him. "Sometimes when I was a cub, and my littermates couldn't decide what game to play or where to go to practice hunting, Winter would have us vote. There were four of us, so sometimes it was a tie, but at least we all felt like we'd had our say."

"That's a great idea!" Rain said. "That way, we'll know what everyone thinks, without having to listen to them argue about it all day."

"And it'll be fair," Leaf added, nodding slowly. "Some pandas probably won't like the decision, but if it's what most of us want to do, they'll understand."

Ghost hoped she was right about that.

They made their way to the feast clearing, gathering bamboo as they went, and soon the Feast of Sun Fall was upon them. Ghost recited the blessing along with his sisters, looking around as he did at the gathered pandas. Several of them looked nervous, shooting the Dragon Speakers anxious glances. He was quite surprised that they managed to wait until everyone had eaten before Bay piped up.

"Speakers, have you had a chance to think about what we're going to do?" she asked.

Leaf, Rain, and Ghost looked at each other, and then Leaf stepped forward.

"We're going to have a vote," she said. "If more than half of us want to leave, then we'll find our own territories. If not, we'll stay here."

The pandas muttered to each other, some in shocked tones and others with excitement, but none of them questioned the plan.

Leaf picked up a piece of bamboo and dragged it into the center of the clearing.

"If you want us to leave the Prosperhill and split up," she said, "stand on my left. If you want to stay, stand on the other side."

A few pandas immediately chose sides. Azalea looked up to see she was standing next to Blossom on the left side of the bamboo, and sniffed derisively, but didn't change her mind. Other pandas joined them.

Five to leave, and none to stay . . .

Ghost held his breath as he watched them, thinking for a moment that it was going to be a quick and decisive vote for the pandas to split up. But then pandas started to move to the other side too: Rain's adoptive mother, Peony, was the first.

Five to three . . .

Dawn and her cub Frog joined the right side, and Fir trotted happily after them, sticking beside her friend. But then she gasped as she turned and saw that Horizon and Cypress had both gone to the left.

"Mother," she said, "Father, why are you over there? We're staying here! Aren't we?"

"Come over here, Fir," Cypress said.

"No!" Fir squeaked. "I'm staying where I am!"

"Speakers," Horizon said, "Fir is just a cub, she has to stay with her family."

"Every panda gets to have a voice," said Rain firmly. "Even the cubs."

Horizon and Cypress looked at each other in dismay.

Seven pandas to six...

Ten to eight... it's going to be close...

Crag moved toward the right, and when he got there he turned and looked back at Lily. She took a deep breath, looked down at her paws, and then went to the left. Crag said nothing, but he looked as if she had sunk her claws into his back.

That meant...

Ghost sat still, looking from left to right, counting and recounting, a sinking feeling in his chest. There were eleven pandas on the left, nine on the right, and the only pandas left were the three Dragon Speakers. Before Ghost could move, Leaf and Rain both immediately went to the right, with the pandas who'd chosen to stay.

Ghost counted again, hoping he'd been wrong—but he hadn't. There were eleven pandas on each side of the bamboo line. And that meant that his was the deciding vote.

He felt the stares of the Prosperhill pandas on him as he tried to think. He wished he'd made his choice earlier. It wasn't fair that they'd left him to make this decision for the whole Prosperhill!

But there was a reason he hadn't stepped confidently along with his sisters. How much did he actually want to stay here? Some of these pandas had called him a monster. It had made him desperate to please, to fit in, and Dusk had taken advantage of that.

"What do you think the freak will do?" some panda

whispered, from the left side of the clearing. He was pretty sure it was Ginseng.

It might make sense for them to disperse after all. He could take Shiver and they could go back to the mountain.

But then he saw Rain and Leaf looking at him, and he made up his mind. He had only just found his sisters. He couldn't leave them yet.

He stepped to the right.

A sigh of relief passed through the pandas on his side of the bamboo cane, and huffs of frustration through the group on the other side.

"So it's decided," Leaf said. "We will stay in the Prosperhill together."

"Wait, no! That's not fair," said Azalea. "So we all have to stay just because Ghost wants us to?"

"Me and eleven other pandas," Ghost pointed out, with a frown.

"It's not Ghost's fault," snapped Rain, to Ghost's relief. "He just happened to vote last. Blame me and Leaf if you want to blame someone."

"Still," Lily said, "why should we have to stay just because the other side got one more vote? Why shouldn't those of us who want to leave set out on our own?"

"And go against the decision of the Dragon Speakers?" gasped Bay.

"Do you really want to leave that badly, Lily?" said Crag, in a quiet voice.

"It's what's right," Lily said. "I think you know it too. You can come with me! Our cub can grow up on its own territory, with just us to share its bamboo."

"But we don't know what's out there! What if we run into trouble when the cub's just born?" Crag countered.

Ghost watched in dismay as the bamboo cane rolled back and forth across the ground, as pandas crossed it to argue with each other.

"If you want me to go with you, you'll have to carry me," Fir said to her parents.

"If we voted to stay, we should all stay," said one panda.

"But why? It'll be better for everyone if those who want to leave just go," said another.

"We didn't settle it at all," Leaf said, in a voice only her siblings could hear. "We might have made it worse."

"There's no harm in pandas leaving if they choose to," said Rain. "We just made everyone make their choice, and those who voted to leave can leave, and it'll be fine."

But Ghost didn't think it would be as simple as that.

"Does this have something to do with the Dark Sun vision?" Leaf wondered.

"I guess it could," Ghost said. He meant it to sound reassuring, but it wasn't at all.

A movement caught his eye in a tree at the edge of the clearing, and he looked up to see Shiver sitting on a high branch, her spotted white tail dangling. She leaned her chin on her paws and blinked at him.

Ghost looked back at the chaos unfolding in the clearing, and headed for Shiver's tree. Leaf and Rain seemed too preoccupied with what was going on to notice him slipping away. He clambered up beside his littermate, and she leaned over and gave him a soft lick on the side of his face.

"That didn't go so well," she said.

Below them, several of the pandas were obviously coming to the conclusion that they would simply leave, despite the vote. Not all of them—Ghost suspected that some were staying simply to continue the argument. But a few were going. One of them was Lily. Ghost watched as she tried to persuade Crag, then tried to get him to forgive her, but he turned away, brokenhearted. Lily walked off into the forest, all alone. Azalea left too, and so did Granite. Horizon and Cypress were still arguing.

"Do you remember that time we voted on which way to go hunting," Shiver said, "and all three of us voted to go up, but you wanted to go down? And you sulked about it for days?"

Ghost opened his mouth to say that this wasn't the same at all, but then closed it again. Perhaps he should have known that losing a vote wouldn't make anyone very happy.

"This is what comes of living so close together, by the way," said Shiver. "I agree with the pandas who stood on the left— even though that includes Blossom and Ginseng. Too many pandas in one place is always going to lead to arguments."

Ghost gave a deep sigh. "I know," he said, under his breath, even though he was sure the other pandas were too far away to hear him. "I . . . I very nearly voted to leave. I miss the mountains, and not having to worry about all these other pandas all the time. But I can't leave, I'm a Dragon Speaker; I have to be with the others. Right?"

Shiver just blinked her pale eyes at him.

Ghost bowed his head. "I think I might have made the wrong decision."

"It probably would have gone badly whatever you did," Shiver said, draping her tail over Ghost's paws in a way that he thought was probably supposed to be reassuring. "Do you see what I'm seeing over in that corner?"

Ghost followed the pointing of her nose, and found himself watching Blossom and Ginseng, who were gathering leaves and sticks.

"They're rebuilding their nest," he said. "They're *staying*."

"Strange, isn't it?" Shiver said. "They make a lot of fuss about sharing their space, then they have the perfect opportunity to leave . . . but they don't. Why?"

Ghost stared at the two big pandas, wondering exactly the same thing. What were they up to?

Shiver tucked her tail back over her own paws and fixed Ghost with a hard stare.

"I'd be very careful of them, if I were you."

CHAPTER THREE

"WHAT DO YOU THINK'S happening now?" Quicktail asked, holding her long golden tail in her hands as the band settled down on the ashy ground around Brawnshanks's favorite broken tree.

Nimbletail shrugged at her sister. "It could be anything," she said. It was a safe, noncommittal thing to say, as well as being true. After everything she'd seen Brawnshanks do to the pandas—from blackmail and intimidation, to helping Dusk keep Rain and her mother in a prison pit—she was sure it wasn't going to be anything good. But beyond that, she couldn't guess.

"Shh, he's speaking!" said cousin Swingtail, giving Nimbletail a light shove.

Brawnshanks had stood up on his back legs and opened his

arms wide for a moment, calling for silence among the gathered monkeys.

"My friends," he said. "Every day we grow closer to domination of this land, to the end of the Dragon Speakers and the dawn of the Age of the Monkey!"

The assembled monkeys whooped and cheered and slapped their hands on the ground. Quicktail and Swingtail joined in, and Nimbletail did, too, with as much enthusiasm as she could muster. She saw Crookedclaw perched on a lower branch of the splintered tree, and shivered as her eyes scanned the crowd, probably looking for any monkey who wasn't celebrating with the rest. Nimbletail clapped a little harder.

She couldn't be the only monkey who didn't like Brawnshanks and didn't want anything to do with his plotting against the Dragon Speakers. She just couldn't be. But any monkey who expressed feelings like that would find themselves in deep water—perhaps literally. If Brawnshanks, or *any* other monkey, ever found out that she'd helped the pandas escape from his prison pit in the Southern Forest . . . she didn't know what he would do, but she feared it would be worse than simply killing her.

There had never been so many monkeys living in the same place before, and Nimbletail had never felt so alone.

"The strongest and most cunning among you will therefore be chosen to join the Strong Arms, my elite band of warriors."

A ripple of gasps and excited coos passed through the crowd. Swingtail's eyes went as wide as gingko fruits.

"To choose the new Strong Arms, I have decided that we will hold a competition. A special round of the Three Feats."

Another round of oohing and aahing passed through the crowd. Nimbletail said a dutiful "ooh" along with them, but she also narrowed her eyes. She supposed Brawnshanks could do that, if he wanted—after all, it was always the troop leader who set the Feats. But she'd never known him to run *extra* Feats. Usually they'd take place once a year, as a chance for young monkeys to prove they were adults now, and a way to decide leadership within the smaller family bands. It was complicated, but it was always the same, and as far as Nimbletail knew, it was the same among every species of monkey in the kingdom, and even beyond.

"All will be able to take part," Brawnshanks said, with a wide sweep of one arm, "but only the monkeys with the most cunning, the greatest perseverance, and true ruthlessness will be able to complete the tasks and be chosen to join my Strong Arms."

Several of the monkeys in the crowd jostled and poked at each other. Somewhere over by the ashy trunk of a nearby tree some monkey declared herself the *most* ruthless and a fight immediately broke out. Nimbletail and Quicktail looked at each other and rolled their eyes.

Brawnshanks let the chaos reign for a moment, then held up his hands for silence. A few monkeys didn't immediately notice, and were shaken into silence by their bands.

"Competitors will work in pairs," he said. "To test their

loyalty. Now go, choose your challengers!"

With that he jumped from his perch in the tree and was lost to Nimbletail's sight in the crowd. Bands began to split off, running into the trees or leaping into branches. Each band had between three and twelve monkeys in it, mostly relatives, although sometimes monkeys would leave their family band and join one with mates or old friends.

Nimbletail's band gathered around. Quicktail and Swingtail were joined by their elderly uncle Flicktail, and Swingtail's mate Goldback, with tiny Duskback clinging to her fur.

Swingtail's eyes hadn't stopped gleaming since Brawnshanks had started speaking, and Goldback had a similar excited sparkle in hers as she transferred Duskback from her underbelly to the top of her shoulder.

"You realize what this means," Swingtail said. "If one of us can become a Strong Arm, they'll lift the whole band up with them!"

Nimbletail nodded morosely. It was true—the bands of Strong Arms were lifted to a status within the troop only just below the Strong Arms themselves. They had better food, better trees to sleep in.

And the only price is that one of us has to do Brawnshanks's dirty work, Nimbletail thought.

"Now that the troop is so huge," Flicktail said, "it would be a great boon to have some more influence around here."

"And we have the perfect candidates," Swingtail declared. He hopped between Nimbletail and Quicktail, and threw his arms around their shoulders. "You two make a great team. I know you can do it!"

Quicktail caught Nimbletail's eye behind his back. Nimbletail was sad, but not very surprised, to see that her sister was beaming.

"Let's do it!" Quicktail said. "Think how exciting it would be to be a real Strong Arm! I know *you* got picked to go on a mission to the Southern Forest already," she added, reaching around Swingtail's back to prod Nimbletail affectionately in the arm, "but being a Strong Arm would still be a huge step up!"

Nimbletail tried to smile. If they'd been alone, she might have told Quicktail then and there that her time in the Southern Forest wasn't nearly as fun as it sounded, that Brawnshanks had been a cruel and manipulative leader and his orders always ended up hurting someone who'd done nothing to deserve it. But there was no saying anything like that in front of Swingtail and Goldback.

"What do you say, Nim?" Quicktail prompted.

There was no way to refuse, not without making her band suspicious—or without breaking Quicktail's heart.

"It can't hurt to try," Nimbletail said weakly, even though actually she was sure that it could.

"Your parents would be so proud," said Swingtail, giving both sisters another cheery squeeze.

Maybe, Nimbletail thought. *Maybe.*

* * *

Swingtail's band had planned to arrive early for the First Feat. They'd been told it would begin just after dawn, so they made sure that by the time the sun was peeking over the rim of the mountains, Quicktail and Nimbletail were waiting by the big, twisted pine tree at the edge of the Broken Forest. But there were already six other pairs of challengers there when they arrived, and more turned up while they were waiting for Brawnshanks to appear, their bands taking up places in the trees or on the ground all around them, watching eagerly. Nimbletail recognized a few of the pairs, but there were a lot she didn't know, newcomers who'd made their way to the Broken Forest after Brawnshanks had taken it for the golden monkeys.

Brawnshanks arrived, with Crookedclaw on his heels, as she usually was these days. Nimbletail wasn't sure what her official position was, or if she even had one—she wasn't a Strong Arm, and she wasn't his mate. She was just there, watching and listening.

"It is good to see such enthusiasm," Brawnshanks said, looking out over the assembled challengers from the twisted trunk of the pine tree. "Now we will find out how many of you have the cunning to progress to the Second Feat. Each pair of monkeys must go out into the kingdom and bring back a bees' nest."

"That's an easy one," said a nearby monkey, under his breath. Nimbletail looked around and saw it was a monkey she knew—Briskhand, a male who'd been born in the same summer as her. She knew Briskhand had always wanted to be a Strong Arm. It looked like he was going to get his chance. He'd come with his friend Brightface, whose handsomely vivid blue face was creasing into a skeptical frown.

"I'm not sure," Brightface said. "Brawnshanks never makes anything easy. . . ."

"You worry too much," said Briskhand. "I know where to go, we'll be back here in no time!"

Brawnshanks waved a hand to dismiss the competitors, and the pairs of monkeys scattered in all directions. Briskhand led Brightface out of the clearing with a hooting laugh.

"Good luck!" the bands around them called, waving hands and tails from the trees. Nimbletail turned to look back at her own band, and saw Swingtail and the others waving and cheering as hard as the rest.

"Which way should we go?" Quicktail asked, breathlessly. "We should be smart about this. He said it was a test of cunning, right? Do you know which way the closest bees' nests are?"

"Not sure," said Nimbletail. "I think I saw some bees over there?"

She pointed away from the Broken Forest, in a random direction.

"All right, let's go!" Quicktail said, and bounded off, taking the lead as usual, while Nimbletail followed after her.

They scampered through the Broken Forest, under the splintered and blackened branches of the leaning trees.

Nimbletail hadn't chosen their route particularly carefully, so she shuddered as they found themselves scrambling up the gray slope of loose shale where Nimbletail knew Brawnshanks had almost killed the white panda and his tiger friend. But at last they reached the top, and Nimbletail looked out with relief on the ordinary Northern Forest.

Tall, golden-leaved gingko trees crowded some of the slopes, and squat, curving pines grew along others. Bamboo sprouted in thin patches between the rocks, and long ferns carpeted the ground.

Nimbletail and Quicktail ran up into the closest trees and sprang from branch to branch. Nimbletail grabbed and swung from one, waiting to see where Quicktail would decide to go next, looking around in case there were other challengers who'd decided to take this same route. She heard rustling in the trees nearby, but there was no sign of any other monkeys bursting from the branches. That, at least, was a relief.

She just didn't know what to do. Should she sabotage their chances, so that she wouldn't have to serve Brawnshanks? Or should she try to get Quicktail into the Strong Arms so she had an ally there? Would Quicktail and the rest of the band ever forgive her if they found out she'd intentionally failed? What's more, Swingtail was right—it would be a huge boon to the band if they could rise up the troop ranks.

But I truly do not want to be a Strong Arm.

She kept turning these thoughts over in her mind as she hurried after Quicktail, until suddenly she heard her sister's voice in a tree above her head. "Nimbletail! Up here!"

Nimbletail climbed up into the higher branches of the ginkgo she was standing in, and looked along a branch to see Quicktail peering at the next tree, shading her eyes.

"Bees!" Quicktail said. "Look, the nest's right there!"

Nimbletail followed her pointing finger, and found the lumpy egg shape. It was sticking out of the side of a tree, partially built into a hollow. Bees flowed in and out and around it in a busy stream, the low rumble of their buzzing just barely audible from the monkeys' perch on the next tree.

"All right," Quicktail said, flexing her long fingers. "Let's go!"

Quicktail leaped into a run, as if she might jump from the branch right into the cloud of bees. Nimbletail cried "No!" and made a grab for her sister, catching her by the tail. Quicktail yelped as she was yanked back, slipped off the branch, swung for a moment and then dropped down onto the next branch. She looked up at Nimbletail with a confused and annoyed expression.

"What did you do that for? The nest is right there, if we don't get it someone else will!"

"I'm not doing this," Nimbletail said. "We'll be stung all over! There's got to be a better way. Like you said, wasn't it supposed to be a test of cunning?"

"Well, yes," Quicktail said, climbing back up to sit next to Nimbletail. "But what do you suggest? We could throw rocks at it, or hit it with a big stick? But that would still make the bees angry. There's no way to get them out of there, is there?"

Nimbletail opened her mouth to say no, not that she knew of . . . then she stopped.

"Huh," she said. "There might be another way. You remember what Brawnshanks said the task was? *Exactly* what he said?"

"To bring a bees' nest," Quicktail said. "What are you thinking?"

Nimbletail grinned at her sister. "Come on. I've got an idea."

They weren't the first to return to the twisted pine. On the way there they passed a pair of monkeys who had given up, leaving empty-handed with their heads hanging in shame. Near the tree there were four pairs of challengers sitting in triumphant but grumpy silence, chewing on the tasty honeycomb of the nests they'd brought back, and nursing a variety of awful-looking bee stings.

Just as Nimbletail and Quicktail arrived, they saw Briskhand and Brightface presenting a nest to Brawnshanks. Briskhand was covered in stings, so many that one of his eyes had swollen shut, and Brightface was limping. But they both beamed as they placed their nest down in front of Brawnshanks, and the troop leader congratulated them both.

"You are through to the Second Feat," he said. "You may join your bee-stung brethren."

Nimbletail walked forward as they stepped aside, holding their nest out in front of her. Part of her wanted to hold her breath and hope that she'd been cunning enough to make it to the Second Feat, but part of her hoped Brawnshanks would disqualify them both. Their band couldn't blame her if he was unreasonable about this, after all. . . .

Brawnshanks squinted at it, and a thin smile crossed his leathery blue face.

"Here is our bees' nest, Brawnshanks," said Quicktail, with a bow.

"Hey," said Briskhand. Nimbletail looked around to see him pointing to the old, abandoned nest that they had found, long-ago empty of bees, its combs practically translucent with age. "That's cheating!"

Nimbletail shrugged. "We were told to bring Brawnshanks a nest, and we did," she said.

"Oh, come on." Brightface winced. "An old nest doesn't count! There isn't a single sting on either of them!"

"On the contrary," said Brawnshanks. "This is a bees' nest, and I said nothing about stings."

"Indeed," said another voice, uncomfortably close behind them, and Nimbletail twitched around to see Crookedclaw smiling at her. "It shows great cunning. One might say that Quicktail and Nimbletail are the only pair so far to have *truly* completed the task."

Despite her misgivings about Crookedclaw, and about all of this, Nimbletail couldn't help feeling a flush of pride. Briskhand looked like he wanted to bite her, but he just huffed and stalked off to join Brightface in their honeycomb feast.

"Congratulations, you two," said Brawnshanks. "You have passed the First Feat."

"Yes!" Quicktail yelled, leaping with excitement, and then she seemed to remember herself and cleared her throat. "Thank you, Brawnshanks. We won't let you down!"

As they passed him, Briskhand glared at her with his one good eye. "Cheats," he sneered.

"Enjoy your honey, Briskhand," Nimbletail sneered back.

"I won't forget this," Briskhand muttered. "You two won't get through the Second Feat. Not if I have anything to do with it."

CHAPTER FOUR

"CAN I HELP?" LEAF said softly, settling down beside Crag. He didn't look at her, but kept staring out over the forest. He'd climbed up to the top of this hill and was sitting near the edge of a cliff.

"I just wanted Lily to be safe." Crag sighed. "I wanted our cub to be safe. I should have gone with her. . . ."

"I'm sure they'll both be all right," Leaf said. She wished she could say more, but she knew nothing she could say would help. She wasn't sure why he hadn't gone with Lily in the end, but she knew the decision was weighing heavily on him.

Crag and Lily had talked it over for a long time, but even after all that, neither of them had changed their minds. Lily had gone, and Crag was left behind to wallow in his feelings.

The mood in the Prosperhill had barely recovered—it

seemed that no matter which way they'd voted, almost every panda felt betrayed, whether it was by the result, the behavior of the pandas on the other side, or the pandas on the *same* side.

"If you need my permission to go and look for Lily," Leaf said to Crag, "then you have it. But when she's about to give birth she might change her mind. It's probably safer to stay where she can find you."

Crag hung his head and sniffed at the grass between his paws. "I know. I just wish . . . I wish it had been different."

Me too, Leaf thought.

"Leaf! Hey, Leaf!"

Leaf looked over the edge of the rock and saw Pepper below them, waving a paw. "I found somebody who needs your help!"

"I have to go," Leaf said to Crag. He didn't respond, but nodded and went back to staring out across the Prosperhill. Leaf started to climb down to where the young panda was pacing between the trees. "What's the matter?" she asked, as she bumped down into the leaves at the bottom.

"I met a cat," said Pepper. "A manul called Peerless. She's in the Northern Forest and her kittens are hurt."

Leaf sighed. It was so hard to tell whether Pepper was telling the truth. He'd once claimed to be one of the triplets, putting her search for her siblings into terrible danger—but even after all that, she knew he wasn't a *bad* panda.

A Dark Sun will rise, she thought, almost hearing the words in the Dragon's voice inside her head. Could this manul cat's mysterious problem be related to the Dragon's message?

* * *

The trees were sparser and less green on the other side of the river. There were more of the blazing gold ginkgo trees, and the seraya trees with their long, branchless white trunks. But there was a lot less green, and a lot less bamboo. As she stepped out of the shallow water and onto the Northern shore, Leaf couldn't help heaving a small sigh.

She had grown up here, where the air was cooler and the mountains seemed so much closer. The rocky slopes were covered in brush and pebbles. Life hadn't been easy here for the small group of pandas who had stuck together over the long year of the flood. But it had been her home. She could still almost see her aunt Plum walking between the sparse trunks of the trees.

All of a sudden, standing under the shade of the ginkgo trees, a wave of grief passed over Leaf. She had never seen Plum's body, hadn't even known she'd been killed until much later. She'd never had a real chance to mourn her. She knew that Gale and Hyacinth would have made her a good resting place, with the best bamboo and a blanket of white iris flowers. But it hurt that Leaf couldn't be there. She'd never had a chance to say a real goodbye.

She shook herself as Pepper scampered up the bank in front of her and beckoned. "Come on, the cat's den is this way!"

Near the roots of a large ginkgo tree, lazing fitfully in a pile of golden leaves, was a large manul cat with extremely fluffy fur and a deeply grumpy expression.

"You again," she said, when she saw Pepper approaching. "What do you want now?"

"This is Dragon Speaker Leaf!" Pepper beamed. The manul looked over at Leaf, and her demeanor changed. Her eyes went wide and she sat up, wincing, and tucked her fluffy tail over her paws.

"Oh, Dragon Speaker! I didn't expect—I haven't seen a Dragon Speaker since Sunset's day."

"Leaf, this is Peerless, and she's hurt," Pepper said.

Leaf could see that she was. Peerless shifted a little as she sat; something was wrong with one of her back legs, and there was a lump of some kind right on the top of her head.

"What happened?" Leaf asked. "How can I help?"

"Bees," spat Peerless. "Some of those golden monkeys thought it would be fun to climb my tree and throw a bees' nest down right by my den! I can't think why," she yowled. "They looked like they were stung all over by the time they dragged it off. I'm covered in stings, and so are my kittens— Fearless, Flawless, Matchless, come out here!"

A trio of trembling bundles of gray fur appeared in a gap between the roots, and padded awkwardly out into the light. Their eyes were paler and wider than their mother's, so they looked almost perpetually surprised. One of them took a few steps and then sank down on his belly, mewling with pain. Peerless chirruped in concern and hurried over to lick the top of his head, while his brother and sister came farther out to stare at Leaf. Their small bodies were already covered in the thick fur of their kind, but the bee stings were still obvious. One had a red, itchy-looking nose, and one side of the other's face was badly swollen.

"We'll live," Peerless said. "But those monkeys are becoming a real problem."

"Tell me more about the monkeys," Leaf said. Her fur was itching at the thought of them. Their leader, Brawnshanks, had smashed the original Dragon Speaker's stone, thinking it would stop the triplets from taking their rightful place as Speakers. Why he'd done that, Leaf still didn't know! And Rain and Ghost had told her that Brawnshanks had been using Dusk all along.

Why? she wondered. *What does Brawnshanks have planned that means he doesn't want there to be Dragon Speakers anymore?*

"There are so many more of them than there used to be!" Peerless said. "They sleep in that big, horrible blackened place over the ridge, then they come out into our forest to hunt our prey and steal fruit from our trees. And now they're throwing bees around! I don't know what they're up to, but it can't be good. Can you make them go away?"

"Well . . ." Leaf took a deep breath. "The monkeys have as much right to live in the forest as everyone else, so I can't make them go away. But I'll try to find out what they're doing."

She knew it was a pretty empty promise, and Peerless obviously knew it too. She raised a haughty black eyebrow at Leaf.

Behind her back there was a snuffling sound, and Leaf turned around and almost jumped out of her skin with surprise. She was completely surrounded by creatures. Squirrels, red pandas—though there was no sign of Dasher or his family—a goat with black horns that were almost as long as he was tall, another manul cat, a whole family of yellow-furred weasels, a pair of golden takin, and even a gray wolf, who politely kept his distance from the others. All of them were watching Leaf intensely.

"Dragon Speaker!" cried one of the weasels, throwing herself to her belly in front of Leaf. "You have come!"

"Are you going to do something about the monkeys?" the second manul cat asked.

"Throwing bees' nests!" huffed the goat. "It landed right beside me!"

"You were here too?" Leaf asked.

"No, not here. Over there!" the goat tossed his long horns in the direction of the mountains.

"They took more than one bees' nest?" Leaf said slowly, her fur prickling again. She definitely had a bad feeling about this.

"They were all over the place," said one of the squirrels. "Sprinting along branches, peering into our nesting holes . . ."

"And this is just the latest thing," said another weasel. "They take all the fruit from the trees and they never say thank you, and if they catch you, they'll *eat* you!"

"They're not all supposed to live together," snorted one of the golden takin. Leaf winced a little. "But they're occupying the Broken Forest now and I don't know if they'll ever leave."

"How long are you here for, Speaker?" said one of the red

pandas. "My mother wanted to talk to you, but she's hurt her leg and can't cross the river. . . ."

"I . . . I have to get back to the Prosperhill," Leaf said. A chorus of disappointed noises came from the crowd of animals, and Leaf felt something tugging at her heart.

This wasn't right. All these creatures had just as many problems as those of the Southern Forest—maybe more, if this was where Brawnshanks's monkeys were plotting their next move. Did it really make sense to leave them?

"I'll come back soon," she said. "I have to tell my siblings about the monkeys, but we'll work something out." She hoped she sounded more confident than she felt.

Pepper trotted alongside her as she headed back toward the Egg Rocks.

"Everything's very weird right now," he observed coolly. "What are you going to do about the monkeys? And what about all those other animals who wanted to talk to you—when are you going to come back?"

"I don't know," Leaf said. "I need to talk to Rain and Ghost about it."

But as they headed back to the river crossing, with every step she took from the Northern Forest, Leaf felt worse and worse.

There's so much to do, she thought. *There's a whole Kingdom, and it's our duty to take care of it. How can we do that from where we are? How can we be the best Dragon Speakers we can be?*

* * *

"Leaf, you're back," said Horizon, as soon as Leaf stepped into the feast clearing.

"Excuse me," said Goji, "I was waiting here first."

"Both of you hurry up," said a small pika who was sitting nearby, cleaning its small round ears. "I came a long way to speak to Dragon Speaker Leaf."

Leaf sat down with a thump in the grass as more pandas— and some more squirrels, a red deer, and a crane—turned to look at her and began to make their way across the clearing. They formed a disorderly kind of queue, with Goji and Horizon jostling for position at the front of it. Leaf looked around to see that Pepper was gone, and she didn't blame him.

"Of course," she said, deliberately keeping her tone of voice bright, although she was already tired from walking to the Northern Forest and back, and her head ached with turning her thoughts over and over. "I'll do my best for all of you. Did something happen? Where are Rain and Ghost? They could have helped you while I was gone."

"Well . . . I'm sure they'd do their best," said Horizon.

Unease prickled through Leaf's fur again. She didn't like the sound of that. She picked up a stray bamboo leaf and chewed on it while Horizon asked her what she should do about Fir and her refusal to leave the Prosperhill. Goji unhelpfully butted in to say Fir was almost grown and they should leave her behind, before asking Leaf to tell her what she should do about some fish who'd been trapped in a small rock pool when the river receded.

"That *really is* a Rain question," Leaf told her. But Goji wouldn't leave until Leaf had promised to ask the Dragon if she should carry the fish back to the river.

The pika and the deer had questions that were just as reasonable, and just as irritating. The pika asked her questions about the mountains that she couldn't answer, and when she tried to tell him to find Ghost, the pika looked embarrassed and said he was too scared.

"He's part leopard, you know!" he squeaked.

"Nonsense! He's all panda," Leaf retorted, a little louder than she meant to. "He was raised by leopards, but he won't hurt you. He's a good Dragon Speaker!" she added, addressing the whole clearing. "They both are! You don't need to wait for ages to talk to me!"

The animals in the clearing looked at each other, but they didn't move.

"We just prefer your advice," said Horizon, with a wide smile which she probably thought was flattering and reassuring.

After she'd managed to answer most of the questions at least a little bit, Leaf was exhausted, but she still couldn't lie down and rest. She had to find Rain and Ghost and settle this, or it was only going to get worse. She couldn't turn petitioners away, but she couldn't do this by herself, either.

She found the other two sitting together by a large pile of felled bamboo.

"Leaf!" Rain waved. "Just in time. You can help us carry it

up to the feast clearing."

"It was a quiet day," Ghost added, "so we thought we would make sure there's enough bamboo for everyone tonight, so nobody has to go searching for it in the dark for the Feast of Moon Fall."

Leaf wanted to lie down and press her forehead to the ground. They couldn't know how tired she was, or that it hadn't been a quiet day. They'd even been doing something helpful. But she still felt completely worn down by the two of them, sitting and doing whatever they liked.

She sat down heavily on the grassy slope beside them and slumped over her belly.

"What's the matter?" Rain asked.

"I've had a long day," Leaf said. She told them about looking for Crag, about Pepper's message, the journey, the manul kittens, all the creatures of the Northern Forest, and then the crowd waiting for her in the Prosperhill.

"Why didn't they come to me?" Rain said, looking deeply offended.

Ghost bowed his head and said quietly, "It could be worse. At least they don't think you'll eat them." His face took on a weary expression that Leaf didn't like at all. It looked like admitting defeat.

"I'm going up there to give Goji a piece of my mind," Rain said, leaping to her paws.

"Rain, don't," said Leaf. "We're Dragon Speakers—you can't just start a fight because you're annoyed. And you know if you do, they'll come complaining to me about it."

"Well, what do we do?" Rain demanded. "How can we prove to them that we're just as good at this as you?"

"And what do we do about the Northern Forest?" Ghost asked. "If the monkeys are really getting worse, then the creatures there will need us."

"That's right," Leaf said. She took a few deep breaths, thinking about the faces of the creatures she'd spoken to—and the ones she hadn't. She kept thinking about the red panda with the broken leg. Sure, she could travel to see her tomorrow, but would that mean some creature in the Southern Forest wouldn't get the help they needed?

She looked up at her siblings, and it hurt her heart a little, but she had to say what she was thinking. "The Dragon chose all three of us. We could help so many creatures. I . . . I don't think it can be right that we all stay in one place."

"What?" blurted Rain. "What are you saying? That we should split up?" Her frown deepened for a moment, and then Leaf saw it start to change, from angry and stubborn to thoughtful.

"The Dragon gave us each different responsibilities, and the kingdom is so large, how can it be fair that all three of us are here in the Southern Forest?" Leaf went on. She looked at her brother. "Ghost, don't you feel like you're *supposed* to be closer to the mountains, somehow?"

Ghost looked shaken, and didn't reply.

"I felt so strange coming back to the Northern Forest,"

Leaf went on, "but I think it's where I'm meant to be. Rain stays here, by the river, with her family."

"You two are my family too, you know," Rain muttered.

"We've only just found each other," said Ghost. "We don't know anything about being Dragon Speakers—we were going to work it out together."

"I know," Leaf said, and her heart squeezed. "I don't want to leave you two. But I can't help thinking it would be the best thing for the kingdom. I don't know what else to do."

"I do keep thinking about all the creatures who live in the mountains," Ghost admitted quietly. "What if they need help? It's too far to come to find one of us. And I think Shiver would be glad to go home."

Rain looked down at her paws. Then she head-butted Leaf hard in the shoulder. "I wish you were wrong about this."

"We don't have to split up and never see each other again," Leaf said, nuzzling her sister back. "I think we should set a regular time and place to meet, and whatever's happening, we do our best to be there."

"What about Egg Rocks," Rain suggested, looking up and brightening a little.

"Is that okay, Ghost?" Leaf asked. "It'd be farther for you."

"Fine by me," Ghost said, who was also looking much brighter. "How will we know when to meet?"

"What about . . . at the Feast of Dying Light, on the eve of the full moon," Leaf suggested. "We'll always know when that's coming up."

"That sounds great," Rain said, and then looked sad again. "I can't believe we're doing this. It's only been a couple of months since I knew I even had siblings, and now we're splitting up again."

"I just wish we could have been cubs together," Leaf said. "We missed out on all that time, and now . . ."

"Splitting up is the right thing to do," said Rain. "But we don't have to like it. Although I'll be able to spend as much time in the river as I like without you two nagging me," she added, forcing a smile.

"I'll miss you," said Leaf.

"Me too," said Ghost.

They sat in a brief, sad bubble of silence for a moment, the three of them just looking at each other.

Then Ghost said, "We're doing the right thing for the Bamboo Kingdom." He held out his white stone, and it gleamed in the bright orange sunset.

Rain held out her stone too, and Leaf did the same. Her heart was swelling like it might burst, excitement and apprehension both swirling in her stomach. What would it be like to return to the Northern Forest for good, without her siblings, and without Aunt Plum? But she knew that no matter what, these two pandas would always be her siblings.

"For the Bamboo Kingdom," they all said.

CHAPTER FIVE

GHOST PANTED AS HE reached the top of the hill, and his breath steamed a little in front of his face. Shiver walked behind him, keeping pace easily—she might not have been able to beat another adult leopard in a flat-out race, but her lungs were certainly strong enough to match the speed of Ghost's heavier frame.

The ground they trod was still rock and grass, not yet the snow of the real mountains, but it was much colder up in the far northern hills than it had been on the Prosperhill. If Ghost was honest with himself, the chill was something of a relief.

They crested the hill, and Ghost sat down for a moment, taking in the vista that opened up before them. Rising slopes and columns of rock, the long blue shadows of deep valleys, and beyond, the first peaks of the White Spine Mountains, glittering in the early sun. The sight filled his heart with strange, exhilarating joy.

It's all very well living in a place of warmth and plenty, he thought, *but this is where I belong. The open space. The freedom to roam.*

"It's funny," Shiver said, sitting beside him and licking her paws. "I'm glad to be going home but it's going to be quiet after the Southern Forest. At least there are fewer creatures here to pester you," she added, giving Ghost a nudge on his shoulder with the top of her head.

Ghost smiled at her, but her words set a spike of anxiety building in his stomach.

It is much emptier up here, he thought. *What if there's no-one who needs a Dragon Speaker? What if . . . what if they've chosen me to speak for the mountains precisely because there's almost nobody here?*

It was a thought he'd had before, in the middle of the night, when he couldn't sleep for the sound of another panda snoring nearby. What if being Dragon Speaker for the mountains and the stars just meant staying out of Leaf's and Rain's way while they handled the real work?

Would that be so bad? he asked himself, and was surprised to find that the answer was a clear and distinct *yes.*

"What are you thinking about?" Shiver asked. "You've gone very quiet."

"Just . . . wondering where we should head for," Ghost said. "I don't exactly know where we'll make our territory."

Shiver nodded. "I'm sure Snowstorm and Frost would like

a visit, but we need a place of our own. Maybe you can ask the Dragon," she added, with a flash of mischief.

"I think that might be overstepping a little," Ghost said. "If it wants to get involved, it will."

"Well, you're the one that asked the Snow Cat to help you prove you could hunt," Shiver said, stretching her long back and turning to lead the way along the crest of the hill toward the mountain slope. "But I suppose that was before you knew it might really be listening."

They made their way slowly north, winding across the slopes, dipping into the valleys and climbing again, higher and higher each time. The more they ascended, the more Ghost felt at home, even though there was almost no bamboo here, and the bushes he found were tough and woody. He noted where they were, knowing that wherever they decided to settle, he might have to travel some way each day to fill his belly.

At last, as they came upon a pine forest where a light dusting of snow lingered on the sprays at the top of the trees, they also saw some other creatures. There was a flock of blue sheep, with their coats the color of the shadows between the rocks, and a few mountain goats with long curly horns among them. They turned one by one as he approached, their gaze flicking nervously from him to Shiver.

"Hello," he called. "Don't be afraid, we won't hurt you."

One of the goats took a hesitant step forward, and said, "I think I heard about someone like you—are you a panda? Are you the new Dragon Speaker?"

"I am," said Ghost. He tried to sound serious and authoritative, and not give away how giddily delighted he was that they'd heard of him at all, let alone recognized him. "My name is Ghost, and I've come to be the Dragon Speaker for the mountains."

"Oh," said the goat, chewing a thick stem of grass. "The one I heard about was called Leaf."

"I thought there was just one Dragon Speaker," one of the blue sheep whispered to another. "And aren't pandas black and white?"

"My cousin said Leaf gave great advice," said another goat, looking at Ghost through narrowed eyes. "Are you as good as she is?"

How is this happening? Ghost felt frozen for a moment, staring into space, too thrown to be upset. *How can all of this have gotten here before me?*

He took a steadying breath. "Leaf is my sister. We're triplets, Leaf, Rain, and I. We're all Dragon Speakers."

"Ghost is just as good at being a Dragon Speaker as his sisters," said Shiver. "Probably better. He used to live in the mountains, so he understands them. He's even got all white fur because he's so—so at home in the snow!"

That was going a bit far, but Ghost still gave Shiver a grateful smile.

"I promise I will do my best to help all the animals on the mountain," he said. "We're looking for somewhere to make our territory, but you will be always safe and welcome to visit when we find it."

The goats and sheep nodded thoughtfully to each other, as Ghost and Shiver walked on past them. Ghost let out a sigh as soon as they were out of sight.

"They'll understand as soon as you start talking to the Dragon for them," Shiver said firmly.

"Yes, they probably will," Ghost agreed. "But still, I feel like I'd better do that pretty soon. . . ."

The sun was beginning to set as Ghost and Shiver climbed high enough to be walking through soft, thin snow. It was a clear and freezing dusk, and when Ghost looked up he could see the moon and a scattering of stars already, even though it wasn't yet dark. The long shadows, the blazing oranges and pinks of sunset on the high white slopes, and the bright moonlight already shining down gave the mountainside an eerie, shifting brilliance.

They were making their way across a snowy slope toward an icy-looking cliffside, hoping there would be a cave or some shelter there, when Ghost felt the sun warming his back. Then he realized that it couldn't be the sun—he was standing in shadow.

The feeling wrapped around him, just for a moment, and then passed by, ruffling his fur as if some large, warm body had passed over him. It was bearing to his right, down the white slope, not toward the icy cliffs.

He paused, his heart swelling as he recognized the signs of the Dragon's presence, and squinted at the snow. There was something there, on a snowfield a few dozen panda-lengths from him.

"I think we need to go this way," he said, pointing with his nose. "Can you see what that is?"

Shiver turned and followed his gaze, squinting and sniffing. "I think it's a heap of rocks," she said. "And I smell sheep."

"I need to go and take a closer look," Ghost said. Shiver shrugged.

"All right, as long as we get somewhere sheltered for the night," she said. "Remember what Winter used to say about weather like this."

"The brightest stars bring the coldest nights," Ghost said, smiling to himself as he made his way toward the rocks. "I remember."

As he drew closer, he saw that the heap of rocks went deeper beneath the snow than he had realized—the ground sloped sharply down as he walked around them. The top was flat, large enough for a grown panda to sit up on it and look over the slopes of the mountains.

The warm wind stirred the snow around his paws, and he watched as it tumbled into a hole at the base of the rocks. He put his head inside, and then pulled it out again and called to Shiver.

"It's a cave! It looks like a pile, but it's just one big rock cave. Come and look!"

Shiver hurried down the slope and put her nose into the

cave. "That's surprisingly warm," she said.

"It's sheltered from the wind," Ghost said. "It must get the sun on it almost all day. I think this is it, Shiver. This is where we should make our home for now."

He looked around the slope and saw a sheep's head rising above a snowbank and then ducking down again. He padded over and looked down, and saw a small group of young blue sheep speaking urgently to one another. They jumped and went silent when they saw him, but one was bolder than the rest—the one who'd stuck her head up to watch them as they sniffed around the rocks.

"Those are sacred rocks," she said. "The leopard shouldn't stay there. It's the Great Dragon's place."

"Really?" said Ghost, with a feeling of lightness in his chest.

"My grandma told me," said the sheep. "That's where the pandas would go in the old days to receive messages from the Dragon Speaker. They'd sit up on top and then sleep underneath and look at the stars and think about . . . about . . . Dragon things," she finished. "No pandas have come up here since *her* grandma's time, she says."

"Well, I'm a panda," said Ghost. "And I'm also a Dragon Speaker. So I hope it's all right if I stay here for a while."

"A Dragon Speaker?!" gasped the sheep. The rest of her friends *baahed* and stomped their hooves in the snow in excitement. "Wow! I mean, yes! Of course!"

"If you're a Dragon Speaker, maybe you can help us?" said another sheep, in a timid voice.

"Cozy, don't bother the Dragon Speaker right now," said the first sheep.

"But it's a sign!" said the sheep called Cozy. "Dragon Speaker, our herd's grazing ground has dried up. It's been good grass for years—that's what my mum says—but we're hungry, and it doesn't seem to be growing back."

"Should we stay, or should we move on and look for new grazing grounds?" the first sheep said. "Can you ask the Dragon?"

"All right," said Ghost.

He sat down in the snow, and rolled the white stone out from the fold of his paw. The sheep made gentle *ooooh* sounds as he held it out to them, gleaming in the moonlight. He looked up at the stars.

Great Dragon, he thought. *Should these sheep stay, or move on?*

There was no answer from the glittering stars. Ghost hadn't really expected there to be—the Dragon didn't speak to him for most creatures' day-to-day questions, but he thought it was right to ask, just in case. He held his pose, staring up at the stars, while he thought through the sheep's problem.

I have come to a place where there's not much food for me, he thought. *But I wouldn't advise anyone else to do the same.* His thoughts wandered back, as they often did when he was considering a problem, to his life with Winter and his littermates in the mountain den. They had stayed in the same cave to sleep— but if they had only hunted in the same places every day, they would have starved. They had to go to where the food was.

Surely it was no different for the sheep. They weren't used to their food moving around, but now it had, and they would have to adjust.

He looked down into the wide-eyed expressions of the group of blue sheep.

"Your herd should move on for now," he said. "There are other slopes with more grass. You should search them out, and then come back to your old ground after a few moons and see if it's had a chance to renew."

Cozy let out a high-pitched *baa* of excitement. "Thank you, Speaker!" she said.

"Real advice, from a real Dragon Speaker! Let's go and tell the others!" said the first sheep, and the group of them pranced off down the slope, chattering excitedly.

Ghost watched them go, the sheep's words echoing in his mind.

A real Dragon Speaker!

"That was great!" Shiver said, slinking up beside Ghost after the sheep had moved far enough away. "And I think there's someone else over there who'd like a word."

Ghost followed her pointing nose to the shade of a pine tree growing almost sideways out of a rocky ledge, and saw a golden takin. It approached him gingerly, its eyes flicking to Shiver.

"It's all right," Ghost said. "My name is Ghost, and this is my sister, Shiver—she won't hurt you if you come here to see me."

"Oh, good," said the takin. "My name is Sunteller. Are you really the Dragon Speaker? It's just that I have a question. It's about my mate. . . ."

Ghost nodded and settled in to listen to the takin's explanation of its surprisingly complicated love life, a warm feeling in his heart despite the freezing weather.

A few days later, Ghost stepped out of the cave and shook himself, gazing out over the vista of the Bamboo Kingdom below. It would snow again soon—the clouds hung thick and heavy above him, glowing orange-gray, with faint curtains of falling snowflakes just visible farther along the mountain range.

"Dragon Speaker!" squeaked a voice, and Ghost looked down to see a collection of pika sitting in front of him. They bowed, and pushed forward a long bamboo cane with several sprigs of green leaves on it. "For you!" the pika said. Ghost could see that there was a trail through the snow behind them where they had dragged the bamboo from wherever they'd found it.

Ghost's heart squeezed with gratitude—and his hungry stomach growled with excitement—as it had every time some creature had brought bamboo with them over the last few days. Most creatures brought only their problems, but a few had taken it upon themselves to seek out and bring food to Ghost as well. The first time, Ghost had struggled even to say thank you—he'd been struck dumb by instinctive horror at the memory of Dusk using his position to get the others to bring him the best bamboo. Was this the start of a slippery slope, a path that could lead only to corruption?

But he'd never asked for anything, and surely that must make a difference.

Word had apparently spread across the mountain, and more and more petitioners were coming every day. Ghost was thrilled that most of them seemed to trust him. Shiver kept out of the way while prey creatures were around, and had agreed to claim hunting territory far from the Speaker Rocks.

Perhaps he really could do this, and be every bit as good at it as Rain and even Leaf.

The pika were by far the smallest creatures to bring him food, and even with four of them it must have been a heroic effort.

"Thank you, so much. You didn't have to do this, but thank you," he said. "What can I do for you?"

As the pika were about to explain their problem, a thudding noise caught their attention and they sat up, ears swiveling. Ghost looked too, and saw a group of goats running toward him, kicking up snow around them.

"Dragon Speaker!" one cried, as they bounced closer. "We need your help."

Ghost looked at the pika, who huddled together and bowed their little noses to the snow, gesturing for the goats to go first.

"Thank you," Ghost said, hoping that he would be able to do something special for the pika to thank them for this kindness. "What's the matter . . . Gray Mist, isn't it?"

He was starting to get to know the herds that lived nearby. This group was led by two goats he recognized, a mated pair, Gray Mist and Prancing Leaf.

"It's our kids," said Prancing Leaf, tossing her horns anxiously. "They've gone missing."

"They're always off exploring," said Gray Mist. "But this is different, they've been gone too long. They're good, sure-footed kids, but even the lightest treading goat can get lost or stuck when the snow rolls in, and if a leopard finds them . . . Please, can you help us find them first?"

"Of course," Ghost said. "I'll look myself, and I'll organize some other creatures to help. . . ."

"Or maybe your precious Dragon Speaker's hunted them himself," said a voice from behind and above him.

It was sneeringly familiar. Recognition sparked in Ghost's mind with a horrible jolt. He'd hoped to never hear that voice again.

Why? Why them, why now? Ghost asked the Dragon, with a sinking feeling in his chest as if his heart had suddenly been turned to stone and dropped into the river.

He let out a tired sigh and turned around.

"Brisk," he said, looking up at the jutting flat top of the cave. "Oh, and Sleet, too."

Both the cubs Born of Icebound were lying on the rock, looking down at Ghost. The goats startled and backed away, and the pika dug into the snow with squeaks of terror.

As the Dragon Speaker, Ghost told himself, he was the

Speaker for *all* creatures, including ones he didn't like.

But as a cub Born of Winter, whose mother had been their mother's rival all her life, who'd been bullied all *his* life by this horrible pair, he knew that there was no way they were simply here to ask for help.

They weren't quite full grown yet, but they were much bigger than when he'd last seen them, and they looked like they could easily take down the goats if they chose to spring.

Sleet licked his chops. "Don't you know?" he said. "Ghost is a flesh-eater. He was raised by leopards, here in the mountains. He's hunted down goats and sheep and rabbits. If you want to know what happened to your kids, you should check inside this cave. Maybe you'll find their bones."

"That was a long time ago," Ghost said, turning to the goats. Gray Mist gave him a terrified look. "They're right that I was raised by leopards—I didn't know any different. But I only eat bamboo now. Look!" He pawed over the cane that the pika had brought him. But it didn't seem to reassure the goats. They backed away even more. "I haven't hurt your kids. You *can* check my cave, if you like. You'll find nothing but shreds of bamboo."

"It's all right," said Prancing Leaf in a faint voice. "I'm sure the kids have just run off; we'll find them."

Hot panic heated Ghost's nose and he stepped forward. "Don't listen to these two, they have an old grudge—"

"No!" Gray Mist bleated. "It's all right; it's fine. You just stay there, Speaker." And with that, the goats turned and bolted away, as fast as they had come.

Brisk and Sleet burst out laughing behind him.

Ghost slowly turned around, his fur bristling with fury. "What are you doing here?" he snapped. "Get back to your own territory, or I will make you!"

Brisk rolled over on her back, still laughing, her tail thumping the snow.

"What are *we* doing here?" Sleet chuckled, delicately licking his paw. "That's good, coming from a *bear* like you. Pandas don't belong in the mountains. We're not going anywhere."

"Isn't it obvious why we've come?" Brisk said, turning the right way up again, her jaws opening in a toothy, hungry-looking grin. "We're here to ruin your new life."

CHAPTER SIX

"DID YOU KNOW THIS was here?" Quicktail whispered, as she swung her paw across to the next rock and peered down into the deep, misty darkness beneath her dangling tail.

Nimbletail paused, bracing herself between a stalactite and a shelf of jagged stone while she looked around.

"The cave, yes," she said. "But not *this*."

They'd entered through the crack in the ground in the middle of the forest, which broadened as they went deeper. But the place they were now was more than just a cave. They'd followed a twisting network of caverns that seemed to stretch almost all the way underneath the Broken Forest— some parts were claustrophobic holes just wide enough for a single monkey to slip through, others wide and winding tunnels with long, invisible drops or pools of stinking water. The competitors in the Second Feat had been led to a vast cavern, where the walls sloped up sharply and stalactites hung from the ceiling every few monkey-lengths. Their Feat was to cross, using only the stalactites, without falling down into . . . Nimbletail wasn't sure what was down there. It was so dark, her keen eyes could only make out the rock in front of her face, the flashes of movement of monkeys swinging around her, and the terrifyingly blurry shape of the next stalactite. Beyond and below, there was nothing but black.

It was oddly warm down here, and it smelled of smoke, with a strange, horrible tangy aftertaste. Nimbletail didn't like it one bit.

She pulled herself up to cling to the stalactite with all four paws, trying not to imagine how much weight it could take before it cracked and fell.

This shouldn't be too different from jumping between trees—but the darkness made it feel *very* different.

She eyed the distance to the next one, tensed her arms and legs and then pushed herself into a leap, twisting in the air to grab on to a ledge and swing herself over to a perch on the next rock column. A moment later Quicktail flew past her, letting her momentum carry her straight to the stalactite beyond Nimbletail's.

Other pairs of competitors swung around them, some dangling precariously, letting out hoots of terror as they almost fell.

"Brightface!" Briskhand's voice called out from somewhere

up ahead. "Come on, hurry up!"

It's not a race, Nimbletail told herself. *It's a Feat of perseverance.*

Brawnshanks had said nothing about speed—only that any monkey who touched the floor of the cavern would be disqualified.

As if we needed any more discouragement to stay away from that black pit, Nimbletail thought. She looked down as a scuffling, growling noise from below caught her attention, and then quickly forced herself to concentrate on the leap to the next stalactite. She made it to the same one where Quicktail was holding on, and met her sister's eyes around the ridged rock column.

"There's something down there," Quicktail said, her voice shaking. "We're not alone here."

"We just have to get across," Nimbletail said, partly to herself. "Whatever it is, we ignore it and stick together. Okay?"

Quicktail nodded. "It's a long jump to the next one. I'm going to climb to the top for a better angle."

"Good idea," Nimbletail said. She watched as her sister climbed up the stalactite, digging her clever fingers into the cracks in the stone, half disappearing into the darkness. As she was judging the leap, another monkey struck the stalactite they were on and tried to swing around it and keep going, but as he let go of the rock Nimbletail could already see that he didn't have enough momentum. He grasped for the column, but his fingers didn't even get close. He tumbled into the darkness with a shriek. Nimbletail cringed back, pressing her forehead to the rock so she didn't have to see him fall, even though he was swallowed by the dark long before he hit whatever was down there. His shriek cut off abruptly. And then there was another scuffling, snuffling noise from below, a hooting scream, and a chorus of grunting growls.

Up on the stalactites, Nimbletail heard a chorus of gasps and whimpering from the other competitors, who she couldn't see around her.

"Nims!" Quicktail called, and Nimbletail realized her voice was coming from the next stalactite. "I made it! Climb up and jump, it's definitely closer—just make sure you get a good grip."

Nimbletail followed her sister, climbing as high as she could without knocking her head on the rocky ceiling before jumping, the arc of her fall through the darkness bringing her close enough to splay out her paws and grip on to the next spot. A lump of stone struck her between the ribs and she yelped, winded, but managed to cling on.

"All right, I'm going for the next one," Quicktail said.

She leaped, and Nimbletail heard her land with a scramble of claws.

Then she heard the cracking sound, and Quicktail's shriek of fear. Nimbletail almost sensed rather than saw the movement as the stalactite splintered. Down below, the growling thing roared hungrily, its snarls echoing around Nimbletail's head.

She jumped. As she hit the stalactite beside Quicktail she grabbed on to the rock with one paw and her sister's arm with another, then sprang into a second leap.

"Jump!" she hooted, dragging Quicktail with her. She felt Quicktail's muscles bunch as she pushed off, and they flew through the air together, Nimbletail reaching blindly with her free paw and stretching out her feet in front of her. . . .

Her right foot connected first. She closed her toes over a rock ledge and pulled herself and Quicktail up onto the rocky wall.

They both clung there, panting, for a few moments.

"Thank you," Quicktail whimpered. Nimbletail realized that her sister was holding on to the wall with one paw, still clinging onto the shard of stalactite that had come loose with the other.

The growling below them had turned strangely disappointed.

Nimbletail frowned.

"Give me that," she said, taking the stone from Quicktail's paw. She turned, aimed randomly into the darkness, and threw the stone as hard as she could.

There was a thump, and a shriek—but not the shriek of a monster.

"Ow!" said some monkey. "That's not fair, they're throwing things—"

Other voices angrily shushed them, but the illusion was shattered. Nimbletail let out a laugh.

"It's just monkeys down there," she said. "Brawnshanks probably told them to make scary noises to put us off!"

"How did they get down there?" Quicktail wondered. "And how are they going to get out again?"

"Get him out of here," another monkey voice from below whispered, not quietly enough.

"Let's follow them and see," Nimbletail muttered.

"I'm not sure," Quicktail said. "We can't step on the ground, remember? We have to complete the Feat."

"We will," Nimbletail said. "We've made it this far, we can climb after them without touching the floor."

Quicktail frowned, but then shrugged. "All right," she said. "But if it's not interesting we should come straight back up."

Nimbletail led the way, climbing quietly down the wall, finding plenty of paw holds and jutting rock shelves as she went. The darkness was almost total as they got close to the floor, and she was briefly nervous that they might hit the ground without even knowing it. Then she looked down and saw that she could just make out the shifting shapes of monkeys below her, milling around and making growling and scuffling noises.

She shushed Quicktail very quietly, and climbed down to a place where a faint furry shape seemed to be walking straight into the wall. Sure enough, there was an opening—another tunnel.

She managed to lower herself into it, still clinging to the walls and the ceiling, one foot dangling only a few monkey-heights above the ground.

Why am I doing this? she asked herself, as she inched along in the dark. *I should either drop and disqualify myself so I don't have to be a Strong Arm, or get back to the Feat so we don't disappoint the band! What am I doing?*

"Nim," Quicktail whispered, as if she'd sensed Nimbletail's doubt, as she often could. "Let's go back, this probably just comes out near the entrance. We should get back to the Feat."

Nimbletail was about to agree, when she heard a voice. Edging another step into the darkness, she saw a splinter of light that seemed to be coming through a crack in the rock.

"Why don't you climb back," she said to Quicktail. "I just want to have a closer look, but there's no sense both of us being down here."

"All right," Quicktail said doubtfully. "Don't cheat, though, okay? And don't be long!"

"I won't," Nimbletail said, and behind her she heard the sounds of Quicktail hopping and swinging back along the tunnel.

Nimbletail sighed. She looked down at the ground.

It would be so easy just to drop down. Nobody would ever know.

But I told Quicktail I wouldn't. And if we're going to beat Brawnshanks's Feats, I want to really beat them!

She climbed carefully along the wall and peered through the crack.

". . . Another escape attempt," said the voice. It was Crookedclaw. She was illuminated from above by a shaft of light—there must have been a pretty big hole in the ground somewhere far above them. Nimbletail squinted as she tried to make out the layout of the cave Crookedclaw was pacing around, but she couldn't see much to either side—only that the monkey was walking along the lip of what looked like a hole in the rock. She jabbed her finger at Jitterpaws and Heavystep. "Stay here and watch them, or I'll tell Brawnshanks how close they came this time. Understood?"

"Yes, Crookedclaw," mumbled the Strong Arms.

Another prison pit? Nimbletail thought. She shuddered as she thought of the one that Brawnshanks had persuaded Dusk to dig for him in the Southern Forest. It had been awful enough to watch Rain and Peony lying helpless at the bottom of that hole, but down here in the dark, in a pit made of broken stone . . . it must be so much worse.

It's not big enough for a panda—and it's a lot better hidden than the last one. Who is he keeping here?

She listened for a few more moments, her heart in her throat, hoping to catch the prisoner's voice. But then Crookedclaw stalked out of sight, and Nimbletail quickly swung away, afraid that Crookedclaw might emerge into the tunnel at any moment. She scrambled back to the cavern after Quicktail, and didn't relax or slow her climb until she was out past the monkeys still pretending to be monsters, and clambering back up the wall. Her fingers and toes were starting to feel sore from holding on. She paused on a rock ledge where she could sit down, and stared up into dark ceiling of the cave.

Should I tell her? she wondered. *If Quicktail knew—if I could show her right now the way Brawnshanks treats his enemies—maybe she would understand . . . maybe we could work together. . . .*

But she shook herself, throwing off the idea.

She always rushes into things—it would only put her in danger.

She continued her climb, and found Quicktail dangling from a paw hold, within leaping distance of a stalactite.

"Well?" she asked.

"Nothing," Nimbletail said. "You were right. Let's go."

They still weren't quite the last monkeys to make it to the end of the cavern—Nimbletail could hear scrambling and grunting behind them, as at least one pair was making a slow, careful journey across.

They jumped to the stalactite, and then to the next. Every time, Nimbletail cringed and hung on for a moment, afraid she would hear that cracking sound again and they would tumble back to the ground. But the stalactites held, until they came to the final one, and at last Nimbletail could see a little farther, as light filtered through down the tunnel that would lead them to the surface. A ledge on the far wall was the only way into the tunnel, but . . .

"What?" Quicktail breathed, clinging to the stalactite and scanning the ceiling. "We have to jump to there? It's too far!"

It was much farther than the leaps from stalactite to stalactite, farther than the widest jump Nimbletail had ever attempted. The faint trace of sunlight lay temptingly on the corner of the ledge. But they couldn't get to it.

"Did we go the wrong way? We could jump to the wall and climb around," Nimbletail said, but she knew without even looking that it was too far to get anywhere from here except back to the last stalactite. It would be a long way around now, and there were other monkeys in the way.

"This must be part of the test," said Quicktail. She was climbing up to the ceiling, feeling it for paw holds, but she came away shaking her head. "What are we going to do, Nimbletail?"

"Perseverance," Nimbletail muttered. "And we're in pairs, so we must need each other. . . ."

"Wait, I know," said Quicktail. "I can swing you across!"

"What? That's madness," said Nimbletail, eyeing up the distance again.

"No, it's not. Grab my hand. I'll swing you as hard as I can, and then I'll jump, and we'll both get across! It'll work, trust me. And if it doesn't, at least we know we won't be eaten by monsters," she said.

"We might break our heads in the fall, though," Nimbletail muttered. "But I don't have a better idea."

She tried not to think about the drop, or think at all, as she gripped on to Quicktail's hand and let herself dangle.

It's just like hanging from a branch, she told herself. She wished she could squeeze her eyes shut, but she was the one who had to grab and hold on to the ledge, so she just fixed her gaze on the tiny patch of light. *Just like a branch, JUST LIKE A BRANCH . . .* she repeated to herself as Quicktail started to swing her back and forth.

"Ready . . . set . . . GO!" Quicktail yelled, and Nimbletail felt herself being thrown into the air at the top of her swing. She leaned forward, reaching with all her free fingers and toes that weren't clinging on to her sister . . . and with a stomach-turning lurch she managed to get her fingers over the ledge. She braced herself and gripped Quicktail's wrist even tighter as Quicktail hit the wall with an *oof.*

"We did it!" Nimbletail gasped. "Quick, we actually did it!"

"Well done," said a voice. Nimbletail looked up, and her stomach turned over again as she saw Briskhand step out of the shadows of the tunnel. "Shame Brawnshanks will never know it." He aimed a swipe at Nimbletail's head, and she ducked, hitting her forehead on the stone. He bent over and grabbed at her arm, while her head was spinning, trying to pry her fingers from the ledge.

"Get off, maggot-breath!" Quicktail snarled, and scrambled up Nimbletail's back and tried to get onto the ledge. With both her hands free, Nimbletail managed to half pull herself up. Briskhand aimed a kick at her face and she had to dip back down again. But this time Quicktail was there and she was fast, seizing Briskhand's leg and trying to throw him off balance. Nimbletail half climbed, half leaped up over the ledge and wrestled Briskhand to the ground. He rolled her over, almost knocking her and Quicktail off again, but Quicktail jumped over them into the tunnel, and Nimbletail bit Briskhand in the shoulder.

"If I go over, you're coming with me!" she said, through a mouthful of his fur.

"You two cheats will never be Strong Arms," Briskhand yelled.

"You're the cheat," Nimbletail growled, wriggling out of

his grip and standing up. She almost tripped over him, but managed to get into the tunnel beside Quicktail.

"We should shove him over the edge," Quicktail spat.

"Let's just go," said Nimbletail. "He can fail the next Feat all on his own."

She pulled Quicktail with her as she hurried away up the tunnel.

The Broken Forest was usually a strangely dim place, shrouded by clouds, but compared to the long journey in the dark it felt like emerging into bright sunshine. They clambered out of the tunnel onto the side of a big rock formation, and looked down to see Brawnshanks sitting with a group of monkeys—some looking pleased with themselves, others nursing cuts and bruises and looking ashamed.

"Ah, Nimbletail and Quicktail," said Brawnshanks, smirking as they climbed down to join him. "Good. You have not disappointed me. Congratulations, you are through to the Third Feat, one step closer to becoming Strong Arms and bringing honor to your band."

And guarding your prisoners, Nimbletail thought. *Keeping innocent creatures in dark holes in the ground.*

She had worked so hard to succeed at the Feat, and yet Nimbletail was more certain than ever that she never wanted to be a Strong Arm.

CHAPTER SEVEN

LEAF WOKE UP TO the first gray light before dawn. She rolled over onto her back and stretched out all four paws, yawning and wiggling to scratch between her shoulder blades.

She rolled over again and got to her paws, and looked around.

The Northern Forest was pale and beautiful in the early light, mist wreathing the ground between the trees, and the scent of growing things on the air.

And there were already a small group of creatures watching Leaf. A dhole dog and a pair of marmots were sitting nearby, keeping a careful distance from each other, while a jerboa nervously hopped from tree root to tree root on its huge back paws, washing its giant ears with its tiny front paws.

Leaf sighed. She blinked a few times to try to wake herself

up a little more, then smiled at the creatures. "Welcome, friends," she said.

"Good morning, Dragon Speaker!" chirruped the jerboa.

"Good morning to you too," said Leaf. "If you'll wait here while I fetch some bamboo, you're welcome to join me for the Feast of Gray Light."

She turned away and headed for the thin bamboo stand she had noticed on her walk yesterday. The creatures lingered where they were, and when she brought the bamboo back with her they stepped forward and sat or lay around her, just as the other pandas would have done if they'd all been together. She held up the bamboo, looked up at the thin tops of the trees, and thought of Aunt Plum.

"Great Dragon, at the Feast of Gray Light, your humble panda bows before you," she said. "Thank you for the gift of the bamboo, and the wisdom you bestow upon us."

She ate hungrily, pulling the leaves from the bamboo cane and making up little pawfuls of them to crunch down on. The other creatures watched, reverently. The marmots groomed each other, and the jerboa got up and cleaned its ears again.

It is an honor and a joy to be a Dragon Speaker, Leaf reminded herself. *But it also means having to have a strategy so that nobody asks you difficult questions before the First Feast of the day.*

It had taken her several days to get this deep into the Northern Forest, not because she'd walked very far at all, but because she had spent large portions of every day listening to creatures and considering their questions. The Nine Feasts had been a lifesaver—not only because they were important to observe, which of course they were, but because it gave her an excuse to stand and walk around and think her own thoughts for a moment.

After she'd eaten, she listened to the gathered creatures, and tried to help them as best she could, climbing a tree to see if the Dragon had anything to say while she considered whether there was any way to save the marmots' flooded burrow or find the jerboa's lost love.

Then, when she'd given the best answers she could, it was time for her to move on. She walked downstream and uphill, among the ginkgo trees and the sparse bamboo. She paused at the top of a slope as she found herself looking down toward the stony riverbank where she and Dasher had tried to cross the flooded water using a fallen tree as a bridge, when it hadn't even reached all the way to the far side. She'd been so desperate to get across, she could never have imagined how happy she'd be to be back here in the Slenderwood.

The other Northern Forest pandas had found Hollowtree, a more lush and plentiful place to make their home, farther from the Egg Rocks crossing and the Prosperhill. But Leaf didn't think she wanted to go so far. If she was striking out alone anyway, she was content to stay in the Slenderwood. There would be enough bamboo for a single panda, even if she sometimes had to hunt for it.

And there was something else about this place that she'd missed, a sound she heard now that made her heart squeeze with excitement: the laughter of red pandas. Leaves rustled above her head, and she looked up to see several of the dusky red creatures peering down at her.

"Leaf, is that you?" said one.

"Jumper!" Leaf gasped. "Jumper Climbing Far! What are you doing back here, I thought you'd settled with the pandas?"

"Leaf? Leaf's back!" came more red panda voices, and Leaf let out a laugh as more of them swarmed out of the trees and around the trunks to look. More and more Climbing Fars, several Leaping Highs and Digging Deeps, and yes, there was old Runner Healing Heart, the red pandas' healer who had helped her save the pandas after they'd been poisoned by bad water.

And that meant . . .

"Leaf?"

She turned around, saw Dasher Climbing Far, her best friend, and gave a small jump for joy, lifting her front paws from the ground. She hadn't seen him in a month, not since she'd taken up her position as a Dragon Speaker. He scampered over to her and pressed his head into the fur of her neck.

"I'm so happy to see you," she said. "But I didn't know you'd come back to the Slenderwood!"

"We decided we quite like to roam," Dasher grinned. "We spend some of our time at Hollowtree, and some of it here. We even went up to the mountain—well, the Climbing Fars did. Part of the way," he admitted, with a chuckle. "It's so good to see your face, Leaf. Are you all right?"

"I'm great now," Leaf said.

Many of the other red pandas ran up to her and she greeted them all, licking their small heads or letting them wind their fluffy black-and-white tails around her legs. Eventually they stepped back, and Leaf sank down to sit with her back against a tree, letting Dasher chatter excitedly about all the things they'd seen and all the creatures he'd told that the Dragon Speakers were back.

"Are you really all right?" he said suddenly. "You look like you're a long way away."

"I'm fine," said Leaf.

Dasher gave her a stern look, and she sighed.

"I'm very tired," Leaf said. "I love being a Dragon Speaker, but it seems like the harder I work at it, the more I have to do. Everyone has something . . ."

"Speaker Leaf?" said a voice, and she looked up to see Roller Digging Deep standing nervously nearby. "Could I ask you a question?"

Leaf hesitated only long enough to take another deep breath, but Dasher's small face drew into a frown and he turned on Roller.

"Not right now," he said.

Roller frowned back. "Why not? It could have been urgent!"

"But it's not though, is it," said Dasher. "It's about you wanting Hopper Leaping High to be your mate, but she wants you to leave the Digging Deeps and join the Leaping Highs and you don't want to."

Roller gaped at him.

"Everyone knows, Roller," Dasher said. "Speaker Leaf needs to rest now; she'll talk to you about it later. Tell the others, Speaker Leaf's not available for questions until she's had a nap."

"Thank you," Leaf said to Dasher as Roller hurried off. "Please, let them know if it really is urgent then of course they can disturb me, but . . ."

"It'll have to be *very* urgent," Dasher said firmly. "Come on, there's a comfy nest and a bamboo patch a few trees over."

Leaf's heart swelled with gratitude and love for the little red panda. He walked her to the nest and made her lie down in it while he fetched the bamboo.

Leaf didn't remember him coming back—she woke up slowly from a beautiful sleep to find two equally beautiful green, leafy bamboo canes lying beside her.

"Ah, you're awake," said Dasher. He was lying next to the canes, his fluffy tail tucked over his paws. Leaf rolled over and nuzzled her nose into his fur. She'd missed him so much. "You'd better eat up. I put them off as long as I could, but . . ."

He looked over his shoulder, and Leaf saw that sure enough, a queue of animals was forming. They all pretended not to be watching her as Dasher gave them a hard stare.

"It's all right," Leaf told him. "That nap was exactly what I needed. And this bamboo. They can come and talk while I eat, if they want."

She chomped on the bamboo, and smiled to herself as

Dasher immediately turned and started wrangling the waiting creatures. He'd stepped right into helping her, without her even having to ask. She knew that she'd made the right choice coming back to the Northern Forest now—she couldn't have wanted a better friend.

Leaf settled in for a long afternoon of listening and answering questions, and she did her best, even though many of the animals' queries were hard to answer, and none prompted any kind of response from the Dragon itself.

As a large deer bowed to thank her for her advice and walked away from the clearing, Leaf saw that one of the creatures who was still waiting behind him was Lily.

Leaf beckoned her over, feeling a little apprehensive. The last time she'd seen Crag he'd been alone, at the edge of the Prosperhill, trying to pretend he wasn't waiting for Lily's to return. What was Lily going to ask? Was the cub she was carrying all right? Was she feeling guilty about how things had turned out?

"Hello, Leaf," said Lily. She didn't look anxious at all, actually. "I just wanted to say, you know this part of the forest, where can I find the best bamboo?"

Leaf stared at her. "That's why you've come?" she said faintly, looking over her shoulder at the collection of creatures still waiting to ask the Dragon Speaker their questions.

Lily nodded.

Leaf took a deep breath. "Lily, the best bamboo is in the Southern Forest," she said. "Which, incidentally, is where

Crag is too, and he's heartbroken and worried about you. Why don't you just go back to your mate? There was plenty of bamboo in the Prosperhill for everyone even before half of you left! Why are you being so stubborn about this?"

Lily gasped, then frowned. "Well, that's not advice from the Great Dragon, *is it*? That's *your* own thoughts, and you should keep them to yourself in the future. I know what I'm doing. I'll find my own bamboo, and you should think about what you're saying before you say it—you know these creatures think you're speaking the words of the Dragon, don't you?"

Without waiting for an answer, Lily turned with a huff and walked off into the forest.

Leaf looked down at the green stone in her paw, and then screwed her eyes shut and let out a heavy sigh.

She's right, she thought. *It's annoying, but she is. She asked me for advice in good faith, and I let my feelings get in the way.*

She'd thought it was pretty obvious that she was always using her own words, guided—sometimes—by the Great Dragon. But as she looked into the hopeful, slightly anxious face of the red panda who was waiting to talk to her next, she realized that perhaps it wasn't obvious. Perhaps she really did need to be careful what she said. . . .

The rest of her day was just as busy, though she stopped for the Feasts of Long Light and Sun Fall, inviting any creatures who were waiting to join her in the blessing. She tried to shake off Lily's words and have confidence in herself.

But by the time the sun went down, there was something

else bothering her too.

It had started with a blue sheep. Leaf hadn't been too sur-prised to see one, knowing they occasionally strayed from the mountain slopes, but it soon became clear that this sheep had come down from the mountains specially to see her.

"You know, you don't have to come all this way next time!" Leaf added, after she'd given the best advice she could. "My brother, Ghost, has returned to be Dragon Speaker for the mountains. And he understands much more about living there than I do."

The sheep had scuffed its hoofs in the leaves. "Yes, I know," she said. "But they say . . . well, I shouldn't . . ."

"What do they say?" Leaf demanded.

"He—he's living with a snow leopard, and two other snow leopards have come to join them, and they're all hunting and eating the animals that come to him for help!"

Leaf's heart sank.

She knew it couldn't be true. She knew that Ghost would be hurt to his core if he knew such things were being said about him. But a tiny part of her wondered if something had gone wrong—some accident, or Shiver being careless about where she hunted?

But . . . two other snow leopards.

Could they be his other littermates, Snowstorm and Frost? Could they be hunting close to where Ghost was living, fright-ening off the mountain creatures? Surely even snow leopards would know better?

"Ghost wouldn't hurt another creature," Leaf said, with absolute certainty. "He's a panda, just like me. We're all the Dragon Speakers for the predators, too—maybe they came to ask his advice, and someone got confused. I promise, you can talk to him. We left our home in the Southern Forest so that animals wouldn't have to travel so far to find one of us."

Was it all for nothing? Leaf wondered, as the blue sheep left to begin the long walk home.

She sincerely hoped the sheep would be the only one from the mountains who'd come to her instead of going to Ghost— so she was disappointed when a hog badger approached her and began to talk about her problems with her cubs, back in the Southern Forest.

Leaf tried to tell her that Rain was still there, and was just as good at giving advice as she was, but the hog badger just wasn't having any of it.

"Rain is a lovely panda," she said, "but she's not wise like you. She's always swimming in the river, or busy with panda things. I heard you actually hear the voice of the Dragon!"

"So does Rain!" Leaf said, trying her very best not to snap. "I've seen her do it, she sinks under the water and that's where she hears the Dragon talking."

"Pardon me, but that's what she *says* happens," the hog badger sniffed. "But we all know she loves to be in the water. How can we know she's telling the truth?"

Leaf had to pause and take a long, steadying breath.

It would probably be easier to argue against if she hadn't

occasionally felt the same—perhaps Rain spent a little too long enjoying herself, and not as long as Leaf did on her duties—but she still hated to hear that creatures had started to think her sister was actually *lying.*

Especially if it meant that they were going to keep crossing the river to come to her instead. Leaf wondered how many of the creatures she'd spoken to today might have been from the mountains, or the Southern Forest, and just hadn't mentioned it?

"Rain is a Dragon Speaker," she told the hog badger. "I give you my word, and my advice is that you tell everyone who asks that the Dragon wants you to take your problems to Rain, not me."

The hog badger muttered to herself, but took her advice, and wandered off.

"I don't get it," said a voice, and Leaf looked around to see Dasher sitting beside her. "I mean, *I* think you're the best one," he added loyally, "but they can't expect you to be a lone Dragon Speaker, not when the Dragon picked three of you!"

"Maybe there's something wrong," Leaf said. "There must be some reason they're not getting to do their duties. Maybe we weren't supposed to split up after all."

"Or maybe Rain and Ghost just aren't pulling their weight," Dasher muttered.

"No, that's not fair," Leaf said. "I know they want to, it's just . . ."

She couldn't finish that statement—she didn't know *what*

it was keeping her sibling from doing their duties the way she was.

Dasher made sure that Leaf could have another nap before the Feast of Dying Light, and she made herself a comfortable perch in the crook of a tree and fell asleep at once, only waking up when the twilight was well settled in, as she heard the sound of Dasher's raised voice.

"Hey, stop!" he was saying. "The Dragon Speaker can't see you! She's asleep! Come back after the next Feast and she'll be happy to—are you listening to me? Stop!"

She opened one eye and looked down. Dasher was circling a group of small creatures who waddled determinedly up the slope to the tree where she'd been napping.

The small creatures were pangolins. Leaf had met one or two before, and had thought they were mostly solitary creatures, so she was surprised to see six of them approaching her tree. Dasher was powerless to stop them—each time he tried to get in front of them they simply parted like water around a rock, walking their strange, rolling walk on their two back legs, their long front claws folded neatly in front of their chests. They stopped under Leaf's branch and looked up, as one.

"Dragon Speaker Leaf," a pangolin said. "We are the Children of the Dragon, and we need to speak with you."

Leaf stopped pretending to be asleep, sat up and peered down at the pangolins. Their bright black eyes seemed to gleam at her.

"The Children of the Dragon?" she asked.

"We are descended from the Dragon itself," said the pangolin. "We are not Speakers, but we read the patterns."

"Sorry, Leaf," said Dasher. "I tried to stop them, but . . . they insisted."

"It's all right," said Leaf with a yawn, sliding down from her perch. She landed between the roots of the tree, and bowed to the pangolins.

"And what can I do for you, Children of the Dragon?" she said.

"Oh, on the contrary," said the pangolin. "We are here to help *you*. The Bamboo Kingdom faces a difficult time. A *dark* time. Please, come with us."

Leaf hesitated, looking into the pangolin's eyes. They were quite different from the huge, glorious, whiskered, colorful spirit she had met in the Dragon Mountain. And yet, there was something about the way this pangolin spoke.

The Dragon's words echoed in Leaf's head.

A Dark Sun will rise. . . .

"I'll come," Leaf said. "What do you want to show me?"

"We don't know yet," said the pangolin. "The pattern will tell us."

And then, without waiting for Leaf, the pangolins turned as one and began to trot back down the hill.

Leaf and Dasher exchanged puzzled looks, but Leaf shrugged. "Sounds interesting. Let's go!"

She followed after the group of pangolins, with Dasher at her heels. At first, she couldn't tell where they were leading—they seemed almost not to know themselves, stopping to sniff around at the ground or to send one of their number clambering up into a tree. But at last, they all gathered around a splintered stump. Leaf sat down, close by but hoping she wasn't in their way, and watched as all the pangolins formed a circle around the stump.

"What are they doing?" Dasher whispered.

Leaf simply shook her head and shrugged.

The pangolins hooked their long claws into the stump and started to pull it apart, revealing a swarming termite nest inside.

"Oh, come on. Have they just come here to eat?" Dasher muttered.

But the pangolins didn't eat the termites. They sat back and watched them. As Leaf kept looking, she saw that each pangolin seemed to be following a stream of termites, their noses making strange little circles in the air.

"The pattern," Leaf said. "He said, 'the pattern will tell us'. . . ."

Sure enough, after a short time of watching the termites, the pangolins turned slowly to gaze at Leaf, their expressions somber, and Leaf's happy fascination turned to chill worry.

"What did you see?" she asked.

The pangolin who seemed to speak for the rest stepped forward, his claws clacking together nervously.

"The monkeys," he said. "You must stop them, Dragon Speaker."

"What are they up to?" she asked. "The Dragon told me that a Dark Sun will rise—is this something to do with that?"

"The Dark Sun, yes," said the pangolin. "But more, and worse. The monkey leader is close to his goal. He is going to destroy the Great Dragon."

CHAPTER EIGHT

GHOST LAY IN THE snow on the top of the Speaker Rocks, his chin resting between his paws and his breath slowly melting the snow in front of him into slush.

It was quiet. It had been quiet for a few days now. There were no sheep on the hillside, no foxes coming through to ask his advice. The pika had run away and not come back.

"What are we going to do?" he said. "They haven't just stopped coming here for advice, they're avoiding us altogether!"

Shiver looked up from her spot on a lower rock, her whiskers twitching with concern.

"They'll be back," she said, with a confidence in her voice that Ghost didn't see in her expression. "Two stupid leopard cubs can't keep all the creatures of the mountains away from you. They need their Dragon Speaker."

"But they don't know that," Ghost muttered. "And anyway, there's three of us. If they think I'm dangerous, they'll just turn to Rain and Leaf. And then they'll have to walk so far it'll actually *be* dangerous!" he added. "How can I ever become a good Dragon Speaker if the animals are too frightened to ask my advice?"

"We ought to deal with Brisk and Sleet," Shiver muttered.

"No violence," said Ghost sharply. "I don't want to solve this with violence. And that means you can't either. We can't fight them. If we fight them, even if they lose, they still win."

"Why is this how they're spending their time, anyway?" Shiver said. "Shouldn't they be off practicing to cross the Endless Maw and make their own way in the world, instead of bothering us?"

"That's been true their whole lives," Ghost growled.

He sat up and turned from the view out over the Bamboo Kingdom, setting his gaze on the Dragon Mountain and the row of peaks in front of it.

I am the Speaker for the mountains, he thought. He tried to focus, to meditate on the long line of rock and snow, to remember how he'd felt that day when he stood in the great cavern inside the Dragon Mountain and saw the flash of scales in the smoke and heard the deep, resounding voice. . . .

Great Dragon, he thought, *I only want to serve you and help the king-dom. Please, send me something. Show me what to do. . . .*

He tried to be patient, waiting with his eyes fixed on the

snowcaps, watching for any kind of signal—perhaps a flock of birds or a well-timed earthquake would show him the way?

But there was nothing.

Feeling a little bit guilty, and a little bit embarrassed, he closed his eyes.

Snow Cat, he thought. *You laid your tracks in the snow for me to follow once before. I know you're really the Dragon, or part of it—but you're the Dragon for the great cats. The leopards follow you. Please, show me how I can . . .*

He paused. Instinctively, he had been about to ask how to defeat or drive away the cubs Born of Icebound. But he didn't want that.

. . . how I can make peace between the cubs Born of Winter and the cubs Born of Icebound? he finished.

He opened his eyes and waited, but there were no mysterious paw prints in the snow, and no warm breath in his fur.

The Dragon Snow Cat wasn't listening. Or perhaps it simply didn't have an answer for him.

He wasn't sure which was worse.

Determined to keep trying, Ghost had decided to sleep out of the cave that night. He'd thought that maybe if they walked to the nearby patch of pine trees and slept in the carpet of needles beneath their branches, they would meet some animal he could talk to, or at least he might wake up in the night to find the stars had something to say to him.

And sure enough, Ghost did jolt awake, but his eyes opened

on to the darkness of a starless night.

He felt as if something had pulled his tail, but by the time he'd rolled up to sit and look over his shoulder, there was nothing there.

What was that? he thought. He peered down at Shiver, wondering if she'd kicked him in her sleep or something, but she was lying too far away, curled into a tight mottled white ball with her big paws firmly tucked beneath her long, bushy tail. *Snow Cat, was that you?*

He shook himself, and took a few steps, trying to see if he could find any stars, but they were all hidden away behind a blanket of cloud. Snow fell softly beyond the trees, a few flakes making half-hearted flurries in the air.

"Shh!" someone said, and Ghost jumped, turning around to look for the source of the voice. He couldn't see it at first, but he thought it was somewhere deeper in the trees.

"It's working," another voice said, and this time Ghost recognized it. That was Sleet. He walked more slowly, careful not to make too much noise as he approached.

"So what do we do now?" said Brisk. "Just hang around getting in his way, until no animal in the kingdom trusts him?"

"No, I've got a better idea," said Sleet.

Ghost's blood boiled as he heard them casually talking about ruining his chance to become a proper Dragon Speaker. He crept even closer, and soon realized the two leopard cubs were sitting farther up the slope, on top of a wide stone ledge which he couldn't climb over, at least not quietly. So instead, he snuck up to it and pressed himself to the rock, right underneath where they were. They didn't see him—Sleet kept talking, a purr of excitement in his voice.

"Ghost's not like other pandas, is he? He knows how to defend himself, at least a bit, and he's got Shiver to help him."

"Right," said Brisk.

"But those *other* pandas, down in the Southern Forest, they're soft. They've eaten nothing but bamboo all their lives. They're too big for most things to hunt, but that means they're careless. They probably let their cubs wander all over the forest, all alone. . . ."

Ghost felt the chill of the stone creep up through his paws, into his heart, as he realized what Sleet was suggesting.

"A panda would make a meal fit for a Dragon!" Brisk added gleefully. "And imagine the look on Ghost's face, when he finds out we've eaten one of his friends!"

"More than one," said Sleet. "After all, if no creature up here is talking to him, how will he know until it's much too late?"

Ghost bunched his muscles, about to spring out from his hiding place and smash these two stupid, *evil* leopards' heads together, never mind what he'd told Shiver about violence—but a desperate flash of hunter's caution stopped him. He was never much of a hunter, but he had learned some things at Winter's paws. *Check the lie of the land. Check the direction of the wind. Think. Don't waste your energy if you're not sure you can take your prey down.*

If he attacked now, they'd have the advantage of the high ground. Before he could climb the rocks they would have had plenty of chances to claw at his eyes or push him off and leap down on him.

He couldn't take them both on alone, then and there. He had to try to surprise them, before they could get away. Despite the panic growing in his heart, he forced himself to back away. Every paw step he took through the softly crunching snow sounded like the distant rumble of an avalanche, but the leopards didn't seem to see or hear him as he searched in the darkness for a way up to the ledge where they'd been sitting.

He had to stop them. His heart pounded and his breath rasped in his chest with the horror of what they intended to do. He wanted to fetch Shiver. She could give him a fighting chance. But by the time he'd done that, it could be too late.

He clambered up a shallower slope and began to silently approach the spot where the two leopards were sitting, sniffing the air, hoping that he would be able to surprise them. . . .

A crunch and crackle of twigs, and a braying of distant voices, split the dark air.

"Leopards!" Ghost heard a sheep's voice cry out. "I smell leopards!"

The flock of sheep charged past Ghost, little more than faint shapes in the darkness, but snorting and stamping fit to wake the Great Dragon itself.

Ghost froze, but Brisk and Sleet didn't. They looked

around with their ears back, and then as one they bounded off the rock and began to dart away through the snowy trees.

No!

Ghost scrambled down after them, throwing himself into the snow, picking himself up and running into the darkness. But he was too slow, and it was too late. They were gone.

He stood and stared for a moment, panic building again in his heart, horror filling his mind.

He wasn't sure if Brisk and Sleet truly could hunt and kill pandas—but they were right that Rain and the Prosperhill pandas wouldn't be expecting them. He thought of little Fir and Frog, old enough to wander and play by themselves but still half the size of the bigger cubs. He thought of Brisk and Sleet creeping up on them. . . .

Rain could protect them, he thought. *She and Pebble and the others could fight off a pair of half-grown leopard cubs. But only if Rain knows they're coming. . . .*

He turned and ran through the trees, scrambling up over rocks, running into and rebounding off a tree trunk in the dim light.

If he could just get to the Speaker Rocks, he could send a message to Rain. That was what the sheep had said, that it was one of the places that pandas could go to receive a message from the Dragon Speaker. He just hoped it would work in reverse.

He'd never given a message this way before. Only Leaf had ever done it at all—just once, she said, when she was in the treetops and the Dragon spoke to her. She'd felt the presence of another panda, and had known they lived far away in the Northern Forest and that, if she chose to, she could pass the message on. It sounded slightly mad to Ghost, but right now he believed, with all his heart, that it would work. It *had* to work.

He burst from the tree line onto the pale snow-covered mountainside and started to bound across it, but after only a few steps his paw struck something hard and he tripped, falling face-first into a snowbank in front of him.

He got back up, looking around to see what it was that had tripped him, and then slowly looked up, his heart sinking, to see where the Speaker Rocks had been.

They had been toppled over, some of them rolled away down the slope. The flat top stone of it had been shoved to one side, fallen onto another rock, and cracked in two. The cave underneath, which had been warm and sheltered, was open to the sky and slowly filling up with snow.

"Shiver!" he called out, sniffing around the cave, but the terror that he might find her crushed inside was blessedly short-lived. She wasn't there. He couldn't see her anywhere. Where was she?

Think, Ghost. What do we do?

Shiver's missing, but I know Rain's in danger.

Ghost ran up to the rocks and climbed up the teetering, broken heap, trying to keep his balance as he stared up to where the stars were hidden behind the clouds.

"Rain!" he cried, out loud. "Please, tell me you can hear me!"

He tried to concentrate. *Great Dragon, help me,* he thought. He tried to picture Rain's face in his mind, the Prosperhill pandas sleeping in their nests, the surface of the river and the face of the moon, but nothing worked. He couldn't feel any kind of connection at all.

"Come *on*," he groaned, and the stone under him tipped up and he slid off into the snow. He sat there, slumped and defeated and furious. "Great Dragon, what do you want from me? Why is this always so hard? All I want is to do the right thing!"

There was no answer from the darkness.

"Well, if you won't help Rain, I'll do it myself," he said, getting up and shaking the snow from his fur. He started to run back down the slope, away from the broken heap of rocks.

He would catch up to Brisk and Sleet, somehow. He would stop them himself. He'd asked the Dragon to help him solve this peacefully, but if there was no other way to save the pandas, then he would stop them by force. He couldn't give up, but he felt so hopeless, as if the whole kingdom was working against him.

"Shiver!" he cried as he ran. "Where are you?"

"Ghost!" came a voice from higher up the slope behind him. He skidded to a stop and turned to see Shiver running out of the trees, close to where he'd seen Brisk and Sleet. "What's going on? What happened to the rocks?" she gasped. "I woke up and you were gone, and then I scented Brisk and Sleet in the forest. . . ."

Ghost growled his explanation, his eyes still fixed on the valleys ahead in case the clouds suddenly cleared and he spotted the two leopards.

"I should have stopped them when I had the chance," he finished. "Now they've slipped away, and I don't know what to do. . . ."

"We'll follow them," said Shiver firmly. "I can still find their scent, if we hurry. If they're hunting pandas, then we'll hunt *them*. Don't worry. They think they're big and clever, but I bet they've never even been beyond the snow line. You'll catch them before they can hurt anyone."

Ghost sighed, and looked up at Shiver, his heart warming as she blinked determinedly at him.

I'm not alone, he thought. *Even if the Dragon isn't here to help me, I'll always have Shiver.*

CHAPTER NINE

NIMBLETAIL'S HEART SANK AS the Strong Arms led them back into the maze of tunnels below the Broken Forest for the Third Feat. She'd hoped never to go back to that dark place. What was this one going to be—swimming blind through a dark, freezing lake? Perhaps the Strong Arms were just going to take the competitors deep underground and let them find their own way back—Nimbletail already knew that they had taken enough turns and passed enough empty cracks in the tunnel that it wouldn't be a simple task.

But something much stranger than cold and damp was starting to happen to the tunnel around her, as she marched on, with Quicktail on one side and the few other pairs of competitors in front and behind. Instead, the tunnel began to feel warm.

How can it be getting warmer, when we've only been walking deeper? she wondered. *Maybe we've walked so far that we're going to burst out at the side of a sunny cliff beside the river. That would be nice. . . .*

But the air grew hotter and hotter, and no less stifling. And all of a sudden, instead of walking in complete darkness, she could see the fuzzy heads of Silvermane and Quickfingers up ahead. There was heat and light.

For a moment she was afraid that Brawnshanks had somehow had his Strong Arms set a fire down here. Then the tunnel suddenly opened up and they stepped out onto a wide rock ledge, and Nimbletail recoiled from the blast of heat.

"One pair at a time, you may approach the edge and look down," said Silvermane.

Nimbletail and Quicktail waited their turn while one other pair went up to the edge—Nimbletail heard one of them, a monkey called Widenose, let out a curse and spring backward.

When Nimbletail looked over, she felt as if the hair on her face was curling in the heat. For a moment she couldn't even understand what she was seeing, until her eyes adjusted to the bright color.

A river of fire, but solid. It looked about the texture of tree sap, but glowing an eerie red-gold and flecked with black ash. Nimbletail squinted, noticing that around the edges of the river, the ground looked almost the same texture, but hardened and still.

It's rock, she thought, dismayed. *Rock so hot it's running like honey.*

Beside her, Quicktail shuddered and pulled something from her fur—a nutshell from their previous meal. She held it over the edge and let go. Nimbletail hunkered down and held on to the nice solid rock under her as she watched it fall, twisting through the air, until it hit the black rock surface beside the river and immediately burst into flame. It burned away to nothing in moments.

"All right, all right, let someone else look," said Silvermane, her impatience undermined by a horrible grin. Nimbletail thought she was enjoying the shock on the faces of the monkeys who'd never seen anything like this before.

Once all the pairs had seen what was below, Quickfingers lined them up and pointed down into the depths.

"That," she said, "is called *lava*. That is why the Broken Forest is like it is. A long time ago, there was a massive earthquake. The lava rose up and burst out of the hole we came in through, and it burned the forest and melted the rocks all around."

Nimbletail stared at her.

I knew Brawnshanks was a little crazy, she thought. *But he's brought every golden monkey to this place—and it's a death trap. A Broken Forest sitting over a river of burning rock. If there was another earthquake . . .*

She tried not to think about it too much.

"And that," Quickfingers said, pointing over the chasm to another dark tunnel opening, "is where you are going."

There were two routes across. Nimbletail spotted them even before Silvermane pointed them out—either side of the glowing chasm, thin rock ledges snaked along the walls. Her mind raced as she realized that both routes were *terrible*. Both involved long leaps, scrambling climbs up sheer rock, and narrow ledges.

Would they have to choose which way to go? Was one of them secretly much worse?

Nimbletail gripped Quicktail's hand and squeezed.

"We'll figure this out," she whispered. "We'll make it across together."

"But before you begin," said Silvermane, rubbing her paws together. "There's just one more thing."

Nimbletail's eyes narrowed.

"What now?" muttered Briskhand.

"This is a test of the final quality Brawnshanks requires in a Strong Arm: ruthlessness. Not only will you want to beat your rival pairs across the chasm, but you also need to beat your co-competitor. The first, and *only* the first from each pair to make it to the other side will become a Strong Arm. The other will have failed."

The hot, sticky atmosphere in the cave took on a chilly quality as one by one the pairs turned to each other. Nimbletail could see most of them sizing each other up.

"No," Quicktail muttered, squeezing Nimbletail's paw again. "I don't want to compete against you!"

If only you knew, Nimbletail thought. "Whichever one of us wins, we'll play fair, okay?" she said.

"Right!" Quicktail nodded.

She gave Quicktail a reassuring smile. *This is a huge relief! You can become a Strong Arm, and elevate the band, and I won't have to!*

The Strong Arms were pulling the pairs apart now, sending one to the left path and one to the right. Nimbletail went to the left.

"You will also fail the Feat if you fall below the ledge," said Silvermane. "And if you fall into the lava—well, I'm sure your companion will let your band know that you died doing your best."

"Good luck," Nimbletail said to Quicktail as they split up.

Briskhand paused near Nimbletail and gave her an unpleasant smile.

"*Neither* of you are going to be Strong Arms," he said. "See you on the other side . . . maybe."

Then he followed after Quicktail to join the group going to the right.

Nimbletail stared after him, her fur crawling—but she couldn't focus on him for more than a few seconds, because she was being ushered off the ledge and onto the start of the precarious path.

"Two . . . one . . . go!" shouted Quickfingers.

Nimbletail fell into her place in the line, trying not to look down at the lava as she put one foot after the other along the thin ledge. Up ahead, the first real challenge loomed: a vertical leap to reach the next section of walkable rock. The jump was twice the height of any of the monkeys—easy, if it'd been a jump from the ground up onto a rock or a tree branch, but the risk of falling into the fiery river made it daunting . . .

"Look out!" said a voice. Nimbletail felt a monkey's paws

grip onto her shoulders and head, pushing her down as one of the other competitors vaulted up from her shoulders onto the higher ledge. She steadied herself with all four paws on the ground, then glared up at the monkey. It was Longfinger. Nimbletail scrambled up after him, afraid that the other monkeys behind them might get ideas about using her as a stepping stone too, and as she pulled herself up onto the next ledge she saw that his cousin Sliptongue was pulling ahead on the other side of the cavern, casting an angry glance over at Longfinger's lead.

Nimbletail tried to focus. All she had to do was get to the other side, and not accidentally beat Quicktail there.

She hopped over cracks in the path that shone red from the bright hot lava below them, and clambered along part of the wall over a gap where the heat from the river blasted her tail and made it swish uncomfortably. She squeezed onto a ledge where the only option was to turn sideways and inch along holding the wall for balance.

There was a shriek just as she was about to step onto safer ground, and she forced herself to hold on, take a deep breath, and get off the thin part before she turned to look.

One of the monkeys behind her was dangling from the ledge by his fingertips. He kicked his legs, frantically trying to find purchase on the rock wall.

"You!" yelled Quickfingers. "Disqualified! Get out of the way!"

Nimbletail could hear the faint sound of panicked cursing as the monkey began to shakily climb back along the wall toward the Strong Arms. If he slipped now . . . Nimbletail turned away, not wanting to be watching if he did.

"I'll get there," one of the monkeys on the other side yelled over. "For our band!"

Nimbletail looked over at them, searching for Quicktail. She was making good progress, but they were still neck and neck. Nimbletail had to slow down.

Nimbletail paused at the edge of another leap, pretending to be scared of the jump, pressing herself to the wall to allow the monkey behind her to pass by. She waited until Quicktail had made her own jump, from the ledge to a rock sticking out of the wall and up onto a higher perch, then she prepared to leap—but at the last moment she caught herself on the wall, gasping in horror.

Briskhand was coming up behind Quicktail, and as she jumped, he made a grab for her tail. Nimbletail's heart dropped into her toes. But Briskhand had missed. Quicktail made it up onto the higher ledge, and Briskhand glared at her and leaped himself. . . .

But he'll try again, Nimbletail thought. *He's going to kill her.*

"Quicktail, look out!" she yelled, but she wasn't sure if her sister heard her.

Nimbletail spun around, coming face-to-face with another monkey.

"Out of the way!" she cried, grabbed the other monkey's shoulders and spun them both so that they swapped places. She didn't stay to listen to the monkey's startled shouts. She ran, climbed, edged, and swung as quickly as she could back along the path.

The others shrieked and yelped as she climbed past them or jumped over them.

"What are you doing?" snapped a monkey called Sharpeyes, as Nimbletail paused, gasping, to press herself against the wall and let Sharpeyes pass.

"Just go!" she shouted.

Sharpeyes shrugged and hurried past her. Nimbletail tried to press on, she was almost back to the start, and she could see the two Strong Arms watching her with disbelief on their faces. . . .

But then someone grabbed her arm.

It was Brightface.

Nimbletail tried to wrestle her arm away from him, but he held on tight, determination creasing his handsome blue face.

"No! Your band will not succeed," he snarled.

Nimbletail stopped pulling and glared at him.

"Did Briskhand tell you to sabotage me?" she demanded. Brightface didn't answer, but his frown deepened. "Do you *really* think Briskhand will give two nutshells for you once he's a Strong Arm? You're an idiot for trusting him. You'll be here holding me back while he's winning this Feat—unless you let me go and stop him."

Brightface's frown melted away. He looked thoughtful for a moment, and Nimbletail made herself wait. Then he let her go, and with a nod he sprang forward up the path.

Nimbletail hurried back, past a few more monkeys, and skidded onto the wide ledge where the Strong Arms were standing.

"You're disqualified," said Silvermane, nonplussed. Nimbletail didn't stop to reply. "You know that, don't you?" Silvermane shouted after her as she mounted the right-hand path and began to scramble up it.

This time she had to put every ounce of speed she could muster into traversing the ledges and jumps, squeezing past other monkeys and leaping over them. She couldn't stop. If she stopped, if she was too late . . .

She made the jump where she'd seen Briskhand grab for Quicktail, and as she pulled herself up to the higher ledge she saw them. The ledge was two monkeys wide, just, and Briskhand and Quicktail were wrestling on it. Briskhand had a grip on Quicktail's neck and was pushing her bit by bit toward the edge, but Quicktail's teeth were buried in his arm, and her knee slammed into his ribs, making him wince and pull back.

Nimbletail leaped and dug her fingers into Briskhand's fur. She wrenched him away from her sister just as Quicktail aimed another sharp kick at his side. She scrambled away from the edge with a panicked gasp and stood for a moment, rubbing her throat, as Briskhand struggled in Nimbletail's grasp.

"Go!" Nimbletail said. "Run!"

Quicktail gave her a terrified look, but then turned and sprinted for the end of the path. It was close now, just across a wide jump and up a final ascent of jagged, jumbled rocks.

Briskhand elbowed Nimbletail in the ribs as she watched her sister go, and Nimbletail let go of his fur with one hand, but she kept a grip on the back of his neck. She stumbled, half-dangling from Briskhand's fur. He cursed her and all her band as he tried to dislodge her fingers and she tried to drag him down to the ground.

"You tried to kill my sister," Nimbletail snarled into his ear. "If you think I'm going to let you be a Strong Arm, you're *very* mistaken!"

Still gripping him, she ducked her head as another monkey landed on the ledge beside them, hooted in shock and then vaulted over them. Briskhand winced as she pushed off his back with her foot.

"I'm *going* to be a Strong Arm," he grunted. "And when you're gone, I'll be able to get my revenge on your sister!"

He gave a great heave and managed to disentangle himself from her. Nimbletail felt the edge of the rock underneath her and the searing heat of the lava on the back of her head. He was going to throw her off. She would fall headfirst. . . .

She tensed every muscle in her body and sat up fast, her head striking Briskhand's in a head-butt that left Nimbletail's own ears ringing and her vision swimming. She fell forward and then scrambled to her paws. Briskhand was holding his head, staggering, yowling in pain—and then his foot slipped on the edge of the rock, and he started to fall.

Nimbletail grabbed for his arm, missed, and managed to

get her hands around his foot instead. She held on tight and braced herself against the rock. There was a loud smack as he swung and hit the rock below, and she felt his foot give a horrible *pop* and the bones moved under her fingers, but she gripped it with all her might.

"Help!" Briskhand screamed. "Don't let go!"

"I'm not going to let go, you big baby," Nimbletail muttered, not really worried about whether he could hear her or not. "I'm not like you." She started to pull him up, until he could get his own fingers into the crevices of the rock. She reached for his hand and gripped it in her own, and as he tried to kick off the wall to get up onto the ledge, a large chunk of stone came free underneath his foot. It tumbled down into the lava river, and an explosion of molten stone spewed from where it hit. Briskhand screamed and Nimbletail turned to shield her eyes as a drop of it struck his tail.

Nimbletail pulled him up onto to the ledge, panting with the effort, and when he was safely on the flat surface she slumped against the wall and tried to catch her breath. The smell of burning fur and flesh tickled her flat nose as Briskhand clutched his smoking tail and wailed with furious agony.

"Disqualified!" Silvermane's voice called. She was standing on the path along the other side of the wall. She pointed toward the tunnel entrance, where Quickfingers had already made it and was tapping her hands impatiently on the stone. "Both of you are disqualified. Now get over there, we don't want to keep Brawnshanks waiting!"

Briskhand glared up at Nimbletail, and for a moment he looked so angry she thought he might attack again and try to throw her in.

He already hated me, she thought. *But now he owes me, too. I think I've made an enemy for life.*

But instead of lunging at Nimbletail, Briskhand simply made a pained, angry noise in the back of his throat and hurried away from her along the ledge, limping on his broken foot and still holding his tail.

The long clamber back up to the surface through the pitch-dark tunnels was cold and awkward, but Nimbletail didn't mind—she just wanted to put as much distance between herself and the lava as she possibly could. They clambered up out of a crack in the earth and emerged into a gray, misty evening, a light rain drifting between the dead trees of the Broken Forest, and Nimbletail turned her face to the sky and let the rain fall on her.

She felt as if a weight had been lifted from her shoulders as she looked over at Brawnshanks, who was surrounded by half of the competitors—the ones who had been the first to cross the chasm. His new Strong Arms. He was congratulating them all, patting them on the back or ruffling the fur on the tops of their heads.

"Nimbletail!"

Quicktail emerged from the group and sprinted over to Nimbletail, throwing her arms around her. They stumbled and danced together for a moment before Quicktail sat back, her eyes wide and glistening.

"You threw away your chance for me," she said. "To save my life. You could have been a Strong Arm. . . ."

"You'll be a much better Strong Arm than me, anyway," said Nimbletail. "I'm glad you won. You would have anyway, if Briskhand had played fair."

"I'm glad Brightface won, too," Quicktail said, looking over at the retreating back of Briskhand, who was slinking away into the trees without congratulating his Feat partner. "He isn't so bad, after all."

"Quicktail, you did it!" came a voice, and Nimbletail saw Swingtail and the rest of their band hurrying over, their tails quivering with excitement. "You're a Strong Arm! This is going to be so good for the band, just wait and see."

"Let's go and get something to eat," said Goldback. "And you can tell us all about the last Feat!"

They ushered Quicktail away, and Nimbletail followed after them, dragging her feet a little. She was happy for Quicktail . . . mostly. She just hoped that Brawnshanks wouldn't force her to do anything too awful. Perhaps it was a good thing—perhaps Quicktail would realize how terrible he was all on her own, and then together they could try to figure out what to do?

She was also exhausted, and shaking a little as the terror of the fight over the chasm bubbled up and then ebbed away. But at least it was all over now.

"Congratulations, Nimbletail."

Nimbletail started, turning to find herself looking into the smiling face of Crookedclaw.

"W-what? I didn't—Quicktail won the Feat," Nimbletail stammered. "Not me."

"Oh, I know." Crookedclaw's hand slipped around Nimbletail's elbow and she found herself being walked to one side, while her band disappeared through the trees.

Being taken aside by Crookedclaw was never, ever good news. Nimbletail's head spun—had Brawnshanks found her out? Was she about to be vanished, thrown in the pit with the other prisoners?

Crookedclaw was still smiling, in her own knowing way.

"Don't worry," she said. "The Strong Arms told us what happened in there. You may not have passed the Feat to become one of them, but you have passed a test today."

CHAPTER TEN

LEAF PANTED AS SHE ran along the valley floor, between tall rock columns. The valley ended in a steep slope up into the foothills of the White Spine Mountains, and Leaf did her best not to slow her pace as she started up the rocky hill. Dasher trotted alongside her, his little legs working hard to keep pace.

Leaf saw her breath starting to mist in front of her muzzle as they climbed higher, and by the time they reached the top there was frost on the grass that covered the slope and a thick mist visible in the valley behind them.

They carried on along the edge of a ridge, and then paused to catch their breath. Leaf looked out over the rolling slopes and columns, searching the landscape, her heart squeezing with worry. Would they be in time to stop the monkeys? Would they even be able to find the place the pangolins had spoken of?

"I wish we could have brought Coiling Cloud with us," she said.

"He wouldn't have been able to keep up, and we couldn't carry him," Dasher said, flopping down on his side and looking up at the mountains.

"I know," said Leaf. "But he's the one who saw this hill, or sensed that it existed, at least. He might have been able to help us."

"Maybe we'll find Ghost," said Dasher. "We're right on the edge of the mountains now."

Leaf hoped so. She didn't know what was happening in the Prosperhill, but if Coiling Cloud was right and the monkeys were about to destroy the Great Dragon at a hill in the mountains that looked like a skull, it didn't make much sense that no one would be told but her. They couldn't be destroying the Great Dragon right under Ghost's nose, could they? She hoped he was on his way to the same place, right now, but her stomach twisted as she thought about it. Brawnshanks could have hurt him, or stopped the message getting through somehow.

"We have to keep going," she told Dasher.

They hurried on, swapping the soft mists of the Northern Forest for crunching frost under their paws and hard scrambles over rocky terrain. Leaf was glad of her climbing skills, and glad they hadn't tried to bring the pangolin, as she led Dasher in scaling a cliff, to save the time it would have taken them to find a way to walk to the top.

At last, she pulled herself up over the lip of the rock and gasped.

There it was, unmistakable.

Thank the Dragon. . . .

Two large black hollows stared out from the side of a hill, like empty eye sockets looking over the Bamboo Kingdom. A smaller hillock in front poked out like the shape of a muzzle, with boulders for fangs, and a sharp gap where a nose would be. It looked just like a skull.

"Hurry," she told Dasher, reaching down to help him over the edge. "Coiling Cloud said we had to get to the top."

The skull-like effect was made even sharper by the fact that the hill was covered in a thin, undisturbed blanket of snow. As Leaf ran up to it and began to climb, she noticed that there were no monkey footprints, no evidence of any other creature here at all—at least, not since the last snowfall.

Could we have beaten them here? What are they planning to do? How will we stop them?

All questions she'd tried to ask the Children of the Dragon, but they had no more help for her. Only that the monkeys would destroy the Dragon, and that the top of the skull hill was where she needed to go.

She ran up the last few bear-lengths and stood at the very top, panting, looking around her.

There was nothing. No monkeys doing secret rituals, no Dragon, nothing. Only the empty white slopes of the mountains, pine trees clinging to the sides of the rocks, and down below the Broken Forest, splintered and ashen.

She turned around, pacing in circles, searching for the sign she must have missed. She scented the ground, pawed away the snow and scented again. She didn't smell monkeys anywhere.

"What's going on?" Dasher asked. "Where are they? Are we too late?"

"No . . . I'd know if we were too late," Leaf said. "At least, I think so. Something else is going on. But what?"

She sat down heavily in the snow, and looked out over the kingdom. The view from the skull hill was spectacular—she could see all the way down to the Northern Forest, and farther. She even thought she caught a glimpse of shine from the surface of the river. Immediately below her, snowy slopes gave way to rock, and then quickly to the strange, undulating ground that made up the Broken Forest. The twisted trees and cracked earth were clearly visible from here.

It was quiet, but it didn't feel peaceful. Something was wrong here. If the terrible thing the pangolins had seen wasn't here now, it would be soon.

"Brawnshanks is down there somewhere," she muttered. "What is he doing?"

"Maybe the pangolins lied," said Dasher darkly. "We don't know they really saw anything in that termite mound!"

"Maybe." Leaf frowned. "But I don't think so. More likely, I misunderstood them, or they misread the signs somehow. This isn't over. I feel as if I can smell it on the wind."

She shuddered, and Dasher leaned his small body against hers.

"I'm just worried they've sent us to the wrong place," she whispered. "What if the Great Dragon is being harmed right now, and I'm up here, too far away to help?"

"I think you would know," said Dasher. "Surely there would be roars and earthquakes and . . . I don't know, fire or storms or something. If you think this place really is important, maybe Ghost will know more about it," he added.

"You're right," said Leaf. She got back up with a sigh, her paws aching from the cold and the long, anxious journey here. "We're in the mountains, he *must* know what's going on. Maybe something bad's happening to him! Let's go find him."

They climbed higher into the mountains, occasionally slipping on snow, stopping to rest again when they came across a weak and pale outcropping of bamboo. There was no sign of Ghost, or of any creatures at all apart from a few whirling birds, until they found a track of hoofprints trodden into the snow, and followed it up and around the crest of a hill to find a herd of blue sheep grazing on tough green grass in the shelter of an outcropping.

The sheep looked around, saw Leaf, and startled—then relaxed again with a chorus of relieved *baa*-ing.

"Hello," Leaf called, as she approached them. "My name is Leaf—I'm the Dragon Speaker's sister. Speaker Ghost. Do you know where he is?"

"Gone," said one sheep, "And good riddance."

Another sheep butted the first one with her horns. "Mind your manners, Snug! This is the *real* Dragon Speaker."

Leaf felt a prickle of unease under her fur.

". . . *gone?*" she said. "Where did he go?"

"South," said another sheep. "In a hurry, too. And he took the leopards with him. We were sleeping in the forest, higher up, when we scented them in the forest with us. They could have killed half of us if we hadn't run!"

"When will he be back?" Leaf asked.

The sheep all looked a little bit awkward. "We don't know," said the one called Snug. "Don't know if he is coming back. After that business with the hunting, no creature up here's spoken to him in a couple of days anyway."

Leaf stared at her. What was going on in the mountains? Why hadn't Ghost been able to bring the creatures round?

She was worried for her brother, but the more she thought about it, the more her worry and confusion slowly sank beneath a rising tide of *anger.*

Why was she the only sibling who seemed to be able to do their job? Why hadn't he sent the leopards away, if they were causing him so much trouble?

"So he hasn't been giving advice, or answering your questions? He hasn't been speaking to the Dragon?"

"Don't know," said a sheep. "We . . . we've been avoiding him. Just in case," she added, with a wince. "We know he's a panda, but . . . he's not a *normal* panda, is he? Not like you. Those other two leopards told us he'd been hunting with them, and we couldn't risk it."

"He hasn't hunted anybody," Leaf snapped. She was sure

enough of that, at least. But everything else felt like a pawful of pine needles that had been thrown in the air. What was Ghost doing? Why had he just given up? Where was he now? Did he know anything about the monkeys, or the pangolins, or this attack on the Dragon?

"Thank you," she told the sheep. "You've been very helpful. If you see my brother again, tell him I was looking for him."

"We should trust him, then?" asked Snug. "We'll do it, if you say so."

Leaf hesitated, and then hated herself for it.

"Of course," she said firmly. "Ghost's a good panda, and he wants to be a good Dragon Speaker, if you just give him the chance."

The sheep all nodded and bleated at each other, and Leaf turned away and began to trudge back down the slope with Dasher scurrying at her heels. She felt heavy, as if she was climbing a steep hill instead of walking down one.

I told them they could trust him . . . I just wish I was sure that I could.

There must be a good reason for him to abandon the mountains, let all these creatures believe he was dangerous and simply give up on his duties. Perhaps the Dragon had given him a vision? But what could be more important than saving the Dragon's own life?

She tried so hard to imagine a world where all Ghost's actions made sense, but the more she thought about it, the more fearful she became.

Ghost, where are you?

What if the pangolins had it all wrong—what if the terrible danger they'd seen wasn't the destruction of the Great Dragon itself, but of the Dragon Speakers? If Ghost abandoned his duties, it wouldn't just be him who suffered. The other creatures' trust in all the Dragon Speakers could be lost, forever.

Her paws thumped rhythmically in the thin snow covering the rocky ground as she descended the slope, with Dasher behind her and her thoughts full of Ghost and worry. She stared miserably ahead, not really seeing the ground in front of her paws, until suddenly her eyes focused on something in the snow, and she skidded to a halt with a gasp.

Alongside her own paws as she walked, a sinuous trail was moving through the snow.

She'd seen this before. On the way to the Northern Forest with the Slenderwood pandas and the red pandas, she had seen the pine needles on the mountain displaced just like this—by something long and snakelike. But this time, the dip in the snow was leaving behind a distinct, scaly pattern.

"Great Dragon?" she gasped, watching as the trail slithered off down the slope in front of her. She put on a burst of speed to try to keep up with it, but the Dragon moved faster and faster. Leaf's heart lurched. Was the Dragon trying to run *from* her? "Please," she cried, "Please don't leave me—"

Her cry was cut off in a yelp as the snow underneath her front paws shifted. She tried to catch herself, but the slope took a sudden downward turn and she couldn't keep her balance—instead she rolled head-over-paws, tumbling over and over down the steep slope.

She braced and squeezed her eyes shut as she landed in a snowdrift, expecting a heavy thump and a burst of freezing wet snow in her face. But instead, she felt nothing, as if she hadn't struck anything at all. She looked up at the forest ahead of her, and saw no sign of the Dragon. Instead, the trees seemed thick and dark, with plentiful bamboo sprouting between their roots, but there was no green, only shades of gray. Right in front of her, a single black branch lay fallen on the ground, but as she watched it flared up with bright, white fire. Leaf yelped and tried to draw back as the flame leaped from the branch to the trees and then to the bamboo, until the whole forest was ablaze with pure white flame.

She turned her head and shaded her eyes, and for a moment the white light was so strong that it was all she could see, even behind her eyelids. And then it died.

Leaf opened her eyes as Dasher scampered down to her in the snowdrift. Now she actually was cold and wet, and she got to her paws and shook herself off.

"What happened?" Dasher asked. "Are you all right?"

"For now," Leaf said. She blinked away the afterimages of the blazing white branch. "The Great Dragon sent me a vision. The pangolins were right about one thing. The kingdom is in terrible danger. . . ."

CHAPTER ELEVEN

GHOST PAUSED AT THE edge of the river while Shiver padded carefully across the thick tangle of bamboo canes. He stared over the water at the Prosperhill, his heart in his throat. Brisk and Sleet had beaten them here, but he and Shiver had been gaining all the way. He listened for the terrified cries of panda cubs, or any sign that the cubs Born of Icebound had made their attack, but apart from the constant chatter of birds and small creatures, everything seemed peaceful.

"I think it's sturdy enough," said Shiver, turning in the middle of the bamboo bridge to look back at Ghost. The canes had been caught in a thick tangle, between rocks covered in moss and algae, forming a surface that an animal could walk across to the other side. "But there's a gap here. We'll have to jump it."

Ghost swallowed, and didn't meet Shiver's eyes.

He remembered that awful night on the mountain, when he'd snuck out of the den by himself to attempt to jump the Endless Maw—he'd been so confused and angry and desperate that he'd tried it even though he had never stood a chance of making it across. Pandas weren't built for jumping. He had plummeted down the cliffside, and he'd only been saved because Winter had climbed down to rescue him.

He could still remember the shape of her falling into darkness.

He tried to focus, and judge the distance of the jump in front of him, not the one in his memory. It was tiny in comparison, but he still wasn't sure he would make it. . . .

If I don't try, if we go back and circle around to the Egg Rocks, we could be too late.

"Go," he said to Shiver. "I'll be fine."

Shiver nodded, took a half step back and sprang. The gap was small enough that she sailed over it easily, landing lightly on the matted bamboo on the other side. She ran to the shore and turned to watch as Ghost stepped gingerly out onto the bridge.

It wobbled a little underneath him, but it seemed as if it would take his weight, if he was careful and didn't do anything stupid like jumping up and down. . . .

He paused at the edge of the gap. It was only a single bear-length of rushing water, maybe even less. Under the shade of the bamboo bridge, the river looked dark and deep, as if he could drop into it and fall forever. . . .

"Shiver," he called out. "If I fall in, don't wait for me. I'll find a way to swim to shore. Go ahead and warn Rain!"

"You'll make it," Shiver called back. "But yes, I will."

Ghost took a few wobbly steps backward. He couldn't afford to stand here and worry. Winter would want him to jump. She would want him to help his sisters.

He ran, pushing against the frail bamboo mat, and leaped.

His paws struck down on the other side of the gap. He was so surprised he let out a small yelp and sprinted to the shore in case the bridge collapsed under his weight. Part of it did crack and peel away into the stream, but Ghost made it to the muddy bank and up onto a nice solid tree root, before anything worse could happen.

"Okay, go!" he said to Shiver, and she gave him a proud grin before racing off into the thick tree trunks and grassy hillsides of the Southern Forest. Ghost followed her scent, keeping up as best he could, but knowing she would move faster without waiting for him to find a path. They'd traveled like this all the way down from the White Spine Mountains—Shiver scouting ahead, following the scent of Brisk and Sleet, and looping back to show Ghost where they were headed.

"They went upstream," he heard her call, from a pile of rocks above his head. "No, wait . . . *wait* . . ."

The tone of her voice filled Ghost with alarm, and he tried to spin round to look behind him, but he was too slow. Something slammed into his side and sent him toppling over the

tree roots. He rolled over on his back and landed on a patch
of grass and rock below. Brisk soared over him to land on the
other side, and Ghost just managed to roll out of the way as
the leopard's claws came down right where his muzzle had
been. He staggered up to his paws.

"Shiver, look out!" Ghost yelled.

It was too late. Shiver skidded into view down a grassy
slope on the other side of Brisk, with Sleet stalking after her.
Shiver's side slammed into a tree trunk and she came to a stop,
gasping, seemingly winded. Brisk gave Ghost a horrible grin
and licked her lips as Sleet advanced on Shiver. Ghost let out a
roar of fury and barreled toward Brisk, but at the last minute
he threw himself to one side, his paws splashing through the
water, to circle around Brisk and make a run for Shiver. He
pounded over the pebbles and leaped in front of Shiver just as
Sleet was about to pounce.

Sleet didn't stop but sprang right at him. For a moment all
three of them were falling in a tangle of flailing limbs and
biting jaws. Sleet's teeth closed in Ghost's thick fur, scraping
against his skin. They landed on the riverbank and Sleet and
Shiver sprang apart, yowling.

"I know what you're here to do," Ghost spat, getting to his
paws again and baring his teeth at Sleet and Brisk.

Brisk leaped down from the tree roots, jaws open and claws
bared. Ghost reared up, raised a paw, and smacked at Brisk
with all his might, knocking her out of the air. Brisk landed
in the water with an almighty splash, thrashed for a moment,

and then came back at Ghost as if the river itself had spat her out. Ghost braced to dodge her claws, but then felt pain burst across his back.

"*No!*" yelled Shiver. Ghost instinctively turned, tried to pull away, and felt the sting of skin tearing as Sleet raked his claws down his back. He just had time to realize that Shiver had Sleet by the tail, but he had still gone for Ghost instead of trying to pull away. Then Brisk's claws caught the side of his face and he let out a grunt of pain. He backed away from both of them, out of the reach of Sleet's claws, though he struggled against Shiver's hold to take another swipe at him. Brisk took a defensive stance on the bank, her belly low to the ground, and hissed at Ghost.

"I won't let you hurt the pandas!" Ghost warned her.

Sleet yowled and wriggled under Shiver's grip, Shiver holding him now by the scruff of the neck as if he were a misbehaving cub.

"Come on, then," Brisk said. "If you think you can stop us, then stop us!"

She lashed out. Ghost ducked back. Brisk lunged to Ghost's left, and Ghost realized it was a feint a moment too late—twisting to his right, Brisk managed to catch Ghost across the muzzle, and Ghost felt blood begin to drip down his nose and into his mouth.

But now Brisk's flank was exposed, and Ghost roared and bit down on Brisk's back leg. Blood spattered over his chest and paws as he tore the skin. Brisk howled and slid back into the water. She scrambled away through the shallows, her eyes wide and dark with pain.

"Get out," Ghost snarled. "I never, ever want to see either of you two again—not here, and not on the mountain. Find another territory, or I'll finish you for good."

"Whatever you say, freak," spat Brisk.

Shiver gave a yelp as Sleet suddenly reared up and shook her off—but instead of turning on her, he slunk over to join his sister in backing away.

"Cowards. Go take the leap over the Maw, like actual leopards, instead of bothering the pandas," Shiver said. "And I hope you both fall and break your necks."

The cubs Born of Icebound turned and ran, without another word, Brisk limping on her hurt back leg.

Ghost ran after them a little way, until they reached the bridge of bamboo canes, and then watched as they scrambled over it and vanished into the forest on the other side of the river.

"Good riddance," Shiver said, limping up behind him.

Ghost nodded, but he didn't feel as good about it as he thought he would. Something itched at the back of his mind.

"Why did they come all this way?" he wondered. "They made us follow them across half the kingdom, and for what? A scrap?"

"Huh. You're right—maybe they're just pretending to run away, so they can ambush the Prosperhill cubs later," said Shiver darkly. "We should warn Rain, in case they decide to come back."

"Yes, let's go," Ghost said, but for a moment he still didn't move, just went on staring over the river at the ruffled undergrowth where Brisk and Sleet had vanished.

Something about this still feels wrong. I only got one good bite in, and they ran away. I know they're cowards at heart, but . . .

It doesn't feel like we were winning that fight.

"Rain will be able to take care of the pandas if she has some warning," he said, turning from the river. "We can warn her, and then we can go home."

"Maybe we can sleep, and eat something," Shiver said. "And *then* go home."

Ghost chuckled, and nodded.

They made their way up the panda path to the feast clearing, but before they reached it Ghost realized there was something wrong. The Prosperhill seemed deserted. They didn't see another panda as they climbed the hill, which was strange enough on its own, but there wasn't a single panda in the feast clearing either, and that was almost unheard of.

"Where are they?" said Shiver. "It can't be Brisk and Sleet, can it?"

"Can you scent which way they went?" Ghost asked.

Shiver frowned, and sniffed around the clearing. "There are so many scents," she said. "The freshest ones . . . maybe this way?" She moved toward the south side of the hill. "Yes, I think pandas went this way, not very long ago."

She led the way down the slope, with Ghost following anxiously behind her, until they came upon a cool stream, and Ghost suddenly heard the sound of panda voices.

He hurried up the stream, splashing through the water, Shiver following after him now. They turned a corner, and saw the Prosperhill pandas, gathered around something that lay in the pool of water at the base of a small waterfall. The pandas stepped aside, gasping as they saw Ghost approaching. One of them turned, and Ghost saw it was Rain, standing in the pool beside a black-and-white shape. Rain looked up at Ghost and he saw her eyes were dark and glistening, her face twisted with grief.

The shape in the pool was Pebble. He was dead.

CHAPTER TWELVE

NIMBLETAIL CREPT THROUGH THE tunnels, following her nose and her memory to the cavern where the Second Feat had taken place. She kept to the darker, cooler passages, pausing often to listen for other footsteps or the ring of monkey voices. There was nothing but darkness and silence.

Two questions had kept her awake all through the previous night:

Who is Brawnshanks keeping in that prison pit under the ground? And what does Crookedclaw want with me?

She would find the answers to both before the end of the day.

Crookedclaw had given her directions to a meeting place, and a time to be there, along with instructions not to tell another monkey, not even Quicktail, where she was going.

Nimbletail couldn't help feeling like this was probably a test. The creepy old monkey hadn't said much, but what she had said had given Nimbletail plenty of reason to be nervous:

"You work for me now."

The words echoed in Nimbletail's head, almost as if she could hear them as she made her way through the twisting tunnels.

For a moment, she wasn't sure she'd gone the right way, and then she emerged into a familiar space, dark and dismal, with a bottom wreathed in shadow and stalactites hanging from the ceiling.

She climbed down carefully, and found that the bottom of the cavern was just a mostly flat shelf of stone. Feeling her way around the walls, and only once walking face-first into a stalagmite, she found her way back to the tunnel entrance she'd explored with Quicktail during the task. It almost felt wrong to be walking up it, instead of clambering awkwardly along the walls, but Nimbletail reminded herself that if she wasn't quick and careful here, the punishment would be much worse than being disqualified from the Three Feats.

She peeked through the same crack she had found before, and waited, watching and listening. Sure enough, there was a Strong Arm on duty there. It was one of the new ones, a male she didn't know, who'd won his Feat only yesterday. Nimbletail shuddered, knowing that that could have been Quicktail.

She waited patiently to see what he would do, and eventually, she got lucky. He stood up from his position on the floor beside the pit, looked down into it, stretched, and left the chamber. Nimbletail waited until she heard his footsteps fading down another tunnel, and then slipped around the corner, feeling for the opening. She peeked around the edge of the rock, afraid there was another monkey in a corner of the cavern that she couldn't see from the crack—but no, she was alone in the cave with the pit, and whoever was in it.

The cave was about three panda-lengths across, and about half of it was taken up with the pit. Nimbletail hurried up to the jagged edge, her heart thumping, paused to listen for returning footsteps—there were none, not yet—and looked down into the pit.

As soon as she saw it, she realized she should have guessed. It was a pangolin, probably the same one Nimbletail had heard was brought to Brawnshanks and questioned. She was tightly curled up and seemingly asleep on the cold stone at the bottom of the hole. That would explain the guard leaving his prisoner alone, too—if she was fast asleep, nothing down here should have woken her if he left for a moment.

"Hey," Nimbletail called down into the hole. "Wake up!"

The pangolin startled, and curled tighter for a moment, then raised her head to squint up at Nimbletail.

"I'm here to help," Nimbletail said. "I don't have much time to explain—can you climb out of there on your own? Why are they keeping you here?"

"Go away," said the pangolin. "I'm not falling for any more monkey tricks."

"No, I . . . " Nimbletail began. But what was the point? The pangolin had no reason to believe her, and she couldn't give her a convincing one right now. "I really do want to help you. Just remember that. Most of the monkeys aren't your friends, but I want to do what I can."

The pangolin made a bitter chuckling sound. "Of course. And you can help me, if I just tell you more about the Children. No thank you. Now go away!"

She curled up tight again, until she could have been mistaken for a ridged rock at the bottom of the pit.

Nimbletail sighed, but before she could say anything she began to hear footsteps again.

"I'll be back," she whispered. "You'll see." And with that she slipped out of the cave and back into the darkness of the stalactite cavern. The pangolin's words echoed in her head.

If I just tell you more about the Children . . .

The sun was setting by the time she emerged carefully from the tunnels, looking all around to make sure that she wasn't being watched. She turned the question of the imprisoned pangolin over and over in her head as she made her way back to her band's new tree. What did Brawnshanks want with this pangolin? How could Nimbletail help her escape, without putting Quicktail in danger?

When she got to the tree, Swingtail was bouncing on a high branch, testing its stability. He grinned down at Nimbletail as she approached.

"This is more like it," he said, leaning back into the crook of the branch and letting his tail hang down, curling and swinging happily. Goldback climbed up beside him, with Dustback clinging to her fur.

"So much bigger than our old tree," she said, with an admiring glance up at the higher branches. "And so close to Brawnshanks's own tree! Look, you can see it from here!"

It really was close, with only a few leaning trunks separating them. Flicktail had already climbed up to a high branch and fallen asleep, and Quicktail was sitting on a lower branch and looking up at their new home with awe and a little bit of nervousness.

Nimbletail knew her sister, as well as she knew herself: Quicktail's expression was exactly the same one she always made when she'd rushed into some course of action and was hoping she'd made the right choice. She was probably wondering what her role as a Strong Arm would be like, and whether she would be able to maintain their new status.

"We're moving up in the world," said Swingtail. "And all thanks to Quicktail!"

"And Nimbletail," said Quicktail. "We won the Feats together, remember?"

"With all this space, we'll need a bigger band to fill it," said Goldback. She smiled down at Nimbletail.

Nimbletail sighed. She'd quite like to find a mate, like Goldback was always implying she should. But how could she, with Brawnshanks driving the troop closer and closer to something . . . She wasn't even sure what, but it was something awful, she could feel it in her bones.

"I'll be back again soon," she said. The others didn't really notice, except for Quicktail. Her sister swung down from the branch.

"You've only just got back," she said.

"I want to explore around the tree before the sun goes down," Nimbletail said. She hated how smoothly the lie came out. *Am I even really a part of this band, if I can't tell them where I'm going or why?* she thought.

"All right," said Quicktail, with an uneasy smile. "But hurry back."

Nimbletail waved, and headed off along the edge of the Broken Forest, toward the spot Crookedclaw had told her they would meet. She looked out at the rest of the Northern Forest, its trees sparse but normal, its hills and valleys steep and not ashy and strangely half-melted. She couldn't stop thinking about the river of lava deep underground. How far did it go? Was she standing above it right now? If there was an earthquake, or if the Dragon was angry with them, could it rise up and burn the forest again? If so, what could have possessed Brawnshanks to bring the troop here?

Crookedclaw had been right that if Nimbletail followed the vague directions she'd been given, she would know the meeting place when she saw it. In an otherwise empty and unremarkable clearing, a fallen tree was surrounded by a heap of old broken branches, their leaves rotting on their stems. At a glance it would have looked like any old pile of debris, and no monkey would have bothered looking any closer—but after a short poke around, Nimbletail found the entrance beneath the damp old wood.

She steeled herself before squeezing inside. Whatever Crookedclaw was about to tell her about her new role in the troop, she was sure it wasn't going to be anything good.

At least the inside of the secret den wasn't anywhere near as off-putting as the outside. Dry leaves covered the ground, and the only smells were wood and ash, and not rotting leaves.

Crookedclaw was already there, sitting among the leaves. The light was dim in here, and Nimbletail shuddered at the thought that Crookedclaw had just been sitting here in the dark, waiting, hunched, like a spider in a web. Waiting for her prey to stumble in and be consumed.

"Sit down, Nimbletail," she said.

Nimbletail sat obediently. She didn't want to find out what would happen if she showed any reluctance to follow Crookedclaw's orders. Probably nothing much, not right away. She had never seen Crookedclaw hurt another monkey, never even heard rumors of it . . . but something told her that the slightest disobedience would be stored away somewhere in that sharp mind, like nuts hidden by a squirrel for a cold winter day.

"You must be wondering what your new duties will be, under my command," Crookedclaw said. "It's very simple. You will be asked to fetch things for me—objects, creatures, information. Secrets. You will listen to your fellow monkeys, and to the other creatures in the Kingdom. You might stay here with us, or be sent far away. But everything you do will be vital to making sure that things in the Bamboo Kingdom go the right way—*our* way. Your missions will be secret. You will say nothing about them to your band, or to anybody else. You will report what you find to nobody but me."

Not Brawnshanks? Nimbletail thought.

"So . . . I'm to be a spy?" she said aloud.

Crookedclaw narrowed her eyes at Nimbletail. "How do you think we knew that Dusk was coming back to the kingdom, to try to take his dead brother's place as Dragon Speaker?" she said. "How did Brawnshanks know how to manipulate him, so that Dusk would always think he was in charge, but do everything we wanted him to?"

Nimbletail suppressed another shudder.

"My spies are all over the Bamboo Kingdom," Crookedclaw said. "They live among the other creatures, some openly, some in hiding. They tell me their secrets. I know you were there, in the Southern Forest, when Dusk imprisoned Rain and her mother in that pit."

The bottom dropped out of Nimbletail's stomach.

She knows I helped them get away, she thought. *Of course she does. She knows everything. Is she going to kill me? Put me in the pit with the pangolin? Or maybe threaten to tell Brawnshanks, if I don't do something even worse for her?*

All she could do was nod.

"You're smart. Have you wondered why Brawnshanks hasn't

sent parties of monkeys out to try to destroy any of the triplets since they came into their power? Because they'll be *expecting* it," she said, holding up one finger. "But that doesn't mean the Speakers are safe. Quite the opposite. The triplets will fail, one by one." Crookedclaw's expression took on a quiet, satisfied look, like any other monkey would have after they'd eaten a good meal or woken up from a nice nap in the sunshine. "Ghost will be the first to fall. He should be on the precipice right about now."

Nimbletail nodded some more. She was waiting for the moment when Crookedclaw would accuse her of working against the troop . . . but it didn't seem to be coming.

Interesting, Nimbletail thought, through her subsiding panic. *Perhaps there are some things she doesn't know after all. . . .*

"What's happening to Ghost?" she asked.

Crookedclaw smiled. "That's not your concern right now. I have another job for you first—call it another test. Not that I think you'll have any trouble with it. Your performance in the Three Feats was quite impressive. You were cunning enough to find an empty bees' nest; you were curious enough to throw a rock into the darkness and find out that the monster in your imagination wasn't real; and you were loyal enough to run the course backward, giving up any chance at becoming a Strong Arm yourself, to save your sister. Those are excellent qualities for any monkey."

"Thank you," said Nimbletail. She swallowed. What she was about to say might be the smartest or the stupidest thing she had ever said, and she had no way to guess at which. . . . "One question, if you don't mind?"

Crookedclaw looked surprised, and then gestured for her to go on.

"How do you know you can trust me? Is that what this test is about?"

"Oh, not at all," said Crookedclaw, with a cheery smile. "I already know you'll follow my orders. After all, you've demonstrated that you would risk your own life for your sister, but you wouldn't tell her you were meeting me here. Have you been paying attention? What am I about to say?"

Nimbletail's heart sank. "That if I don't do as I'm told, something will happen to Quicktail," she said, her mouth suddenly dry.

"And not just her," said Crookedclaw. "The rest of your band, too. *Now* do you understand why I trust you?"

Nimbletail gave Crookedclaw a mirthless smile back. "Because I have no choice."

"Good," said Crookedclaw.

Nimbletail just nodded, too numb with fear to panic.

There was no way out now. She could try to persuade Quicktail to run with her, and she might even do it, but Swingtail, Flicktail, and Goldback wouldn't understand, and then Crookedclaw would come for them. . . .

But there was one thing worth holding on to: with Quicktail as a Strong Arm and Nimbletail a spy for Crookedclaw, she was in the best position she could possibly be to find out what Brawnshanks was planning, and stop him before it was too late. Maybe she could help the pangolin escape from the prison pit. And even if it was already too late for Ghost, maybe she could help Leaf and Rain.

Crookedclaw stood up and gestured to Nimbletail to rise too.

"Your first task is quite simple. You and one other of my monkeys are to search the Northern Forest until you find, and bring back, a pangolin."

Nimbletail tried not to startle or give anything away.

They already have a pangolin! Why does Brawnshanks need a second one? Do they think it'll talk if they can threaten one of its own?

"Any pangolin?" she asked.

"No," said Crookedclaw. "In fact we require you to find a very specific kind of pangolin. One of those that call themselves the *Children of the Dragon*. They are a sect: They travel in a group, and they believe that they have visions from the Dragon. Find one of them, and bring them back to us."

Nimbletail could hear the pangolin's voice again. *If I just tell you more about the Children . . .*

"And . . . can I ask why?" Nimbletail said.

"You can always ask," said Crookedclaw. "I will usually refuse to answer. In this case . . . just know that the information the Children supposedly carry is vital to Brawnshanks's great plan."

Nimbletail took a deep breath. "Pangolins aren't small," she said. "I might be able to carry one, but not if it's putting up a fight."

Another smirk of satisfaction crossed Crookedclaw's face.

"That's why you won't be going alone," she said.

Nimbletail turned, and caught her breath as she saw the monkey pushing his way awkwardly through the covering of rotting branches.

"I believe you two have met," said Crookedclaw, with undisguised glee, as the monkey stopped in his tracks and glared at Nimbletail.

Of course.

It was Briskhand.

CHAPTER THIRTEEN

Leaf sat at the edge of the river, watching the Egg Rocks crossing. Sun Fall had passed in a blaze of pink and orange clouds, and now the river reflected back a soft blue sky that grew darker and darker as the Feast of Dying Light approached. Up beyond the hills and tall trees of the Southern Forest, the moon was rising.

Leaf had brought bamboo for the feast, and she rolled the canes under her paws nervously as she waited for the others and thought about her vision.

What was the Great Dragon trying to tell her? Was there going to be a fire, or was the fire just a symbol? What was the spark that would set the Kingdom ablaze? What did it mean that the forest had been all in black and white? What did any of it mean?

She watched the sky, the moon, the river, turning to look behind her in case Ghost hadn't made it to the Southern Forest already.

Dasher was perched on top of some rocks nearby, his eyes mostly fixed on the Northern Forest. Leaf suspected he was looking out for monkeys.

She needed to tell her siblings about the monkeys. She needed to tell them about the pangolins, too, and the skull hill, and she needed to ask them to try harder to make sure the creatures from their territories didn't come to Leaf with their questions—

Not try harder, she told herself. *That's too harsh. Probably.*

She needed to know the truth about Ghost's departure from the mountains. She needed to know if Rain had had any more trouble from the pandas who voted to leave but chose to stay. Maybe one of them had some piece of information that would make the pangolins' faulty prediction, her Dark Sun message, and the strange vision of the burning forest fall into place. Maybe they would be only just in time!

She also needed to see her siblings, just to see them. Even if they had no answers for her, even if they were truly being useless lumps and neglecting their duties, she missed them. And she knew they would *want* to help her figure it all out. She was exhausted from walking all the way to the mountains and back, and for apparently nothing.

The sky darkened, and the moon shone brighter, sharp slivers of light dancing on the choppy water around the Egg

Rocks. Leaf stared at it, until she started seeing strange moon-shaped shadows on her vision when she looked away. Was it not quite full? Was she a day early?

She frowned. *Dark Sun.* The moon was kind of like a sun that came out in the dark. Could it be that the Dragon had been telling her something about the moon? But all it had said was that *A Dark Sun will rise*—and the moon rose all the time.

It was Rain who'd been given the moon as part of her territory. Perhaps she would know something. Or perhaps it had nothing to do with the moon, and that's why the Dragon had given the message to Leaf?

It hasn't spoken about a Dark Sun to either of the others, as far as I know. Whatever happens next, do I have to deal with it alone?

The thought made Leaf shudder, and she looked away from the moon to scan the banks of the river again. The shadows under the trees suddenly looked very dark.

Where *were* Rain and Ghost?

"Leaf? I think it's Dying Light now," said Dasher nervously, jumping down from his perch on top of the rocks.

"I think it's past Dying Light," Leaf muttered. "I guess they might be busy with their duties," she said, although a mean little voice in her head answered *not very likely*.

"What do we do, if they don't come?"

"Well, first I'm going to have my feast," Leaf said firmly. "I'm not delaying my meal just because they couldn't get here on time. And when we've eaten we should go to the Prosper-hill," she added. "To check nothing's gone wrong."

And to give Rain a piece of my mind! she thought.

Leaf picked up the bamboo. "Great Dragon, at the Feast of Dying Light, your humble pandas bow before you. Thank you for the gift of the bamboo, and the kindness you bestow upon us."

She started to pull the leaves from the cane and bunch them in her paw, but hesitated before actually eating.

She didn't feel very kind, right now. She didn't feel like giving Ghost and Rain the benefit of the doubt. After all, it wasn't kind of them to leave her waiting, either.

Do they take any of this seriously? she wondered. *The Great Dragon could be destroyed! And either they don't know, in which case what's the point of there even being three of us, or they don't care, in which case . . . maybe I'm better off dealing with this on my own after all.*

She looked up at the branches of the tree overhead.

Great Dragon, she thought. *Why did you show me such a terrible sign? Is there something wrong with . . . with us? Why did you choose us as Dragon Speakers?*

I'm doing my best, and I don't know if it's good enough. If you're showing me what to do, I don't understand. . . .

She watched the leaves shift in the wind . . . and then she startled, dropping the bamboo cane and clutching the leaves to her chest as she realized it wasn't the wind at all. A pair of black eyes glinted down at her from a low branch.

It was a pangolin.

"Hello," she said warily.

Dasher jumped and looked up too, and then he let out a small groan.

"What do you want now? We just ran halfway across the kingdom to get to your skull hill, and there was nothing there!"

The pangolin didn't answer. Leaf opened her mouth to echo Dasher's question, but stopped as she saw the tree branch shake again, and another pangolin emerge to peer down at her—and then another, and another. Pangolins crept from the undergrowth and peeked their long noses over the tops of the rocks.

"Fire!" said one of them. "The Children of the Dragon have seen a great fire in the Northern Forest!"

"The gingkos burn!" said another. "Smoke chokes the air! The red-furred ones perish in the flames!"

Leaf felt as if the world was suddenly spinning around her.

My vision! The Dragon had shown the pangolins the same thing! Except it sounded like theirs was even worse. She glanced at Dasher. His ears had flattened against his skull in alarm.

"The red pandas?" he said. "Do you mean my family?"

"The Children have seen it," said the pangolin. "Dragon Speaker, you are needed."

"Let's go," Leaf said, her voice and her paws shaking with nervous energy. "We have to save the red pandas!"

"Thank you, Dragon Speaker," said the pangolin, and a squeaking chorus of pangolin voices echoed her words. "Thank you."

"Thank you!"

"Thank you, Speaker!"

The pangolins vanished into the dim shadows one by one,

and Leaf finally stuffed her pawful of leaves into her mouth and stood up.

"Come on, Dash. Let's go!"

Despite the distances they'd already covered, Leaf and Dasher moved through the darkening Northern Forest on light paws, worry following behind them like a strong wind blowing a leaf uphill. They scrambled down the valleys and up the slopes to the higher forest, slipping between the shadows, barely speaking to each other. If the pangolins were right, if the fire was really starting near the red pandas' trees . . .

At last, they came to the top of a hill and Leaf saw the Grandfather Ginkgo, the tallest tree in this part of the forest. The moon shone bright on the gingko trees, and their golden leaves reflected back an eerie pale color—but there was no crackling fire, and she smelled no smoke.

"Thank the Dragon!" Dasher groaned.

"The Children of the Dragon must have seen a fire that *will* happen," Leaf said. *And does that mean that they sent us to the right place before, just too early? Or is there still something else going on?* "We have to warn the red pandas."

They hurried into the trees, and Dasher led Leaf to the first one where red pandas were sleeping in the high branches, like massive red furry berries. He scrambled up the tree at high speed, and Leaf heard him starting to talk about fire as she trotted over to another tree and started to climb. She was tired, but they couldn't waste time—she had to know that the red pandas were safe.

"Wake up," she said. "Hopper, Hunter, Chomper—wake up! We need to move."

Chomper Digging Deep rolled over and almost fell off her branch. "What? Why?"

"There's a fire coming," Leaf said.

Hunter Leaping High sat bolt upright. "A fire?" he gasped.

Leaf took a breath, and considered trying to explain about the Children of the Dragon and their termite-readings and her strange vision, and then said, "Yes. It's not here yet, but you'll be safer elsewhere."

"You heard the Dragon Speaker!" said Hunter, leaping to his paws. "Fire! There's a fire coming! Everybody up!"

Leaf slid back down, satisfied that the red pandas were organizing themselves. If they all just followed her she would be able to take them somewhere they wouldn't be at risk.

I just hope I can find somewhere safe, she thought.

CHAPTER FOURTEEN

RAIN BENT DOWN, SHAKING from head to tail, and began to tug at Pebble's fur. Ghost watched in horror for a moment as she tried to drag him out of the water, and then ran up the stream and put his head down to push against Pebble's shoulder, helping her move the body. There was blood in the water.

"Come on, Pebble," Rain said, gently, through a mouthful of fur. "Come on. You can't stay there. You can't . . ." Her voice cracked. She didn't look at Ghost. Ghost wasn't sure if she even knew he was there.

Lychee hurried up and joined Ghost in pushing, and together the three of them rolled Pebble's body up out of the stream.

"What happened?" Ghost asked Lychee. "Did he fall?"

Lychee didn't answer. Ghost looked at him and caught his

gaze quickly move away from Ghost's face, as if he'd been looking and didn't want to be seen. . . .

With a last push, Pebble flopped onto his back on the soft mossy ground, and Lychee gasped. There were injuries over the front of his chest, and blood on his claws. The biggest, most obvious wound was a single, large bite mark in the side of his neck. Cries went up from the pandas, wails of horror and grief. Peony bowed her head and moaned into her paws.

Rain was shaking her head. "He—he was just—he was at the clearing," she muttered. "He was going to get bamboo for the feast, he was—he was fine. . . ."

Ghost stared at the body. Pebble looked like he must have bled out from the bite. Whatever killed him, it didn't seem like it had tried to eat him.

"I never told him," Rain cried. "I should have told him—he wanted to make up, he was so sorry, and I knew, I knew he was sorry—I forgave him but I never told him! I wanted him to feel b-bad. . . ."

Lychee hurried to her side and pressed his face to the side of her neck, steadying her as she dissolved into wails of grief and horror.

"Ghost," said Goji, stepping forward with a hard, suspicious look on her face. "Why are you here . . . and why are you covered in blood?"

"I came to—" Ghost said.

"To kill Pebble," said Blossom.

Ghost spun around. How could she say that? "Shut up,

Blossom," he snarled, his face turning hot with anger. Blossom flinched.

"We saw him at the top of the waterfall earlier," Blossom said. "And look—he hasn't even bothered to wash Pebble's blood off him!"

Goji and Crag both looked at him with startled fear in their eyes.

It's just like when Dusk tricked me into being his thug. They thought I was dangerous then, too. . . . They'll never truly trust me!

Ghost took a deep breath and forced himself to try to be calm.

"It was Brisk and Sleet," he said. "The leopards. I fought them at the river."

"Leopards? Like *that?*" Ginseng said, and pointed over Ghost's shoulder. He turned and saw Shiver, walking between the pandas, who quickly shuffled aside to give her plenty of space.

"*She* is different. She'd never hurt a panda, and you know it!"

"But what *are* you doing here, Ghost?" said Horizon, putting a paw over Fir as Shiver walked past.

"Brisk and Sleet are bad leopards," Shiver said, her tail twitching. "We were coming to warn you. They came here to hunt pandas—"

Blossom and Ginseng both crowed with something like triumph. "Hunting pandas! You see, she admits that Ghost's leopards are perfectly happy to hunt pandas!"

"They've always been your real family," said Ginseng. "It's

no wonder you went back to your old ways once you'd been alone with them in the mountains."

"This is all pure dung!" Ghost snapped. "We came to warn you!"

"Then explain the white panda we saw on the waterfall!" Blossom retorted. "Is there a second one of you walking around?"

"You must have been *mistaken*," Ghost snarled. "Unless you have another reason to lie. *You're* the only pandas I've ever known who've embraced violence!" Ghost looked around at the rest of the Prosperhill pandas, looking for allies, looking for any hint of sympathy—but even Peony was looking at the blood on his muzzle and his paws with horror. "Everyone knows you worked for Dusk. You tried to kill us on our way to the Dragon Mountain. You almost killed Pepper, too!" he said.

"That's right!" said Pepper, from behind Goji. "I believe him!"

"Shush, Pepper," said Goji, and Ghost's heart sank. If the only panda willing to stand up for him was Pepper, who everyone knew had a loose relationship with the truth . . .

"Rain . . ." he began.

"You were too late," said Rain. The flatness of her voice stung him, deep in his heart. She pulled away from Lychee, and looked Ghost in the eyes. "If you were coming to warn us, then you were too late. Pebble's dead."

"Rain," said Ginseng, "I know we haven't always seen eye

to eye. And he's right, we did serve Dusk, when we thought he was the true Dragon Speaker."

More dung! Ghost thought. *They went on serving him long after they knew the truth!*

"But I'm not lying to you. I saw a white panda on the waterfall cliff, just a little while ago. He wasn't covered in blood then."

"This is all rubbish! Pebble was a good panda, Ghost wouldn't hurt him! You can't be listening to this, Rain!" said Shiver, a hint of a growl in her voice. Ghost shot her a frown, trying to silently tell her to be quiet—but it was too late. The pandas were stepping even farther from them both.

Ghost looked back at Rain. His sister was staring at him, pain and confusion written clearly across her face. She looked down at Pebble, and then back at him.

"Either you killed him, or you failed to save him. Either way . . . you're no Dragon Speaker," she said, her voice cracking. She lies down beside Pebble's stiff, wet-furred body and turned her back on Ghost.

"She's right," said Lychee, with a heavy sigh. "You have no business being a Dragon Speaker. You should give us your stone."

No!

Ghost's paw clenched around the white stone tucked between his pads, and he took a step away. The pandas advanced as he retreated, and some of them had gone from looking sad to looking angry, maybe even ready to fight.

No. This is wrong. Maybe I did fail, but I was trying to help!

He pulled the stone from its hiding place. Then he dropped and rolled it away from him. It bounced through the stream toward Shiver, sparkling and sending up splashes as it went. Pandas made a lunge for it, but Shiver was closer and faster, and she scooped it up in her jaws. She turned to Ghost, frowning with determination.

"Go!" he said. "Keep it safe!"

Ginseng and Horizon barreled past Ghost toward Shiver, but she was already gone, tearing off to the north, leaping rocks and running up trees with a speed no panda could match.

"We'll find her," said Blossom, and she and Ginseng set off into the trees after Shiver, without so much as a glance at Ghost.

"You should go too," said Peony. She stepped to the front of the gathered pandas and stared into Ghost's eyes. Her paws were trembling with emotion, but her gaze was steady and cold.

"Don't worry," said Ghost. "I'm going. I didn't do this," he said, raising his voice—he couldn't see Rain now, but he knew she would hear him. "All of you will realize that one day."

He turned, with as much dignity as he could muster, and began to walk away, following the streambed. He didn't run. He didn't look back. He focused on the grass and the rocks beneath his paws, and the light of the full moon glittering on the water. He kept on walking until he was certain he was out of sight and hearing of the Prosperhill pandas.

Then his paws failed him. He reeled against a patch of bamboo canes and sank slowly to the ground, flumping into a pile of dry leaves, his heart hammering. He stared into the gathering darkness and tried to catch his breath, but couldn't seem to get beyond a shallow gasp.

How did this happen? And how can I possibly put this right?

CHAPTER FIFTEEN

STEAM ROSE FROM THE strange rock formation. A few flakes of snow drifted through the air, got caught in the swirl of the stream, and whisked around and around until they dissolved into nothing.

Nimbletail watched, hunched behind a large stone a little way away from the venting steam. At her elbow, Briskhand was watching too—he was silent, for almost the first time since they'd set out from Crookedclaw's secret meeting spot. Nimbletail felt like she had to keep checking he was still there, still paying attention to the mission, not reaching out to throttle her while she wasn't looking. . . .

She refocused on the steam, and the hunched, scaled creatures who surrounded its source, wobbling back and forth on their stubby back legs. The Children of the Dragon. When the steam billowed one way, they all leaned that way too. When it curled, some of them stretched and curled their fingers. Some of them hummed, and others tapped their long claws on the rock—if there was a pattern to this, Nimbletail couldn't tell what it was.

It hadn't been hard to find them, once they'd found the right creatures to ask. Not many creatures ever came up here, to this exposed, rocky plain between the Broken Forest and the foothills of the mountains. But those who did remembered it well—both the steam rising from holes in the rocks, and the strange little pangolins who lived here.

"What are you waiting for?" Briskhand snapped. Nimbletail sighed. Silence hadn't lasted long, then. She shushed him, and he glared at her. "Well then, I'll go out there and grab one myself!"

He started to shift his weight, and Nimbletail snaked a hand out and gripped his wrist.

"No! Not yet!" she hissed. "I want to know what they're doing!"

"That's not what Crookedclaw told us to do," Briskhand sneered. "Failing to follow orders already?"

"Crookedclaw told *me* to bring her secrets," Nimbletail jeered back. "It's not my fault if she didn't trust you with the same speech."

What am I doing? she thought. *Competing with Briskhand—Briskhand!—to be the best spy? I don't want to be a spy at all! I don't want to have to seize one of these pangolins. . . .*

But there was an element of truth to her hesitation too—she was curious about their strange dance around the steam vent. And it *would* be better to grab one of them alone, rather than barreling into the center of the group and having to deal with them all at once.

Briskhand seemed too busy fuming at Nimbletail to charge in, at least. She tried to focus on the pangolins, and on the steam. More than one had raised their clawed paws to the sky now, and the steam bent and twisted in a breeze that Nimbletail couldn't feel. . . .

Just for a moment, Nimbletail thought she saw the cloud move in a way that seemed strangely . . . *animal*. She could almost imagine that it had a wide head, on a sinuous body, and that it turned its head to look this way and that and then up to the sky . . . but then Nimbletail blinked, and it was gone.

"Great Dragon!" said the pangolins, in thin, reedy voices. "Oh, Great Ancestor!"

"Yes," one said, "the night will come, the night in the day!"

"The darkness will cover the kingdom," said another. "Danger! Danger to the Bamboo Kingdom!"

"Oh, Great Dragon!" cried the others.

"What in the name of the First Monkey are they going on about?" Briskhand demanded.

Nimbletail ignored him. One of the pangolins was splitting up from the others. He clambered down from the rocks and headed toward the tree line, sniffing and snuffling at the ground.

Nimbletail watched with a sinking heart. Perhaps she didn't have to draw Briskhand's attention to it—perhaps if she said nothing, he wouldn't notice, and this pangolin could escape. . . .

"Nimbletail! Are you blind?" Briskhand hissed, digging his elbow into her ribs. "Look, that one's all alone! Let's go!"

He slipped out of the cover of the stone and into the trees. Nimbletail followed him, careful not to make a sound. They crept up on the pangolin, which was depressingly easy—even though they were more than twice his size, he was focused entirely on his scenting. He was looking for food, and he found it, in an anthill teeming with insects, which he started to pick out with his long claws.

Nimbletail waited until he was nosing into the anthill, completely distracted, and then she leaped. The pangolin let out a yelp as she got her fingers around his middle, and tried to wriggle away and run, but Briskhand sprang from the other side and reached out to grab him too. The pangolin shrieked, and Nimbletail's fingers were pinched painfully as he tucked his face into his chest and rolled into a neat ball. Nimbletail yelped and dropped him. But the pangolin didn't uncurl. He stayed in his ball, trembling like a leaf.

Nimbletail and Briskhand looked at one another.

The pangolin was trying to roll away, but he was much too slow. She reached down and gently scooped him up. He was an awkward armful, with his armored plates sticking out, but the pangolin was unresisting.

"I mean, that's one way to do it," chuckled Briskhand. "Come on, let's get back to Crookedclaw." He turned and started to walk off.

Nimbletail felt a desperate urge to let the pangolin go while he wasn't looking—but no good would come of it. With Crookedclaw's threat hanging over Quicktail and the rest of their band, and with Briskhand right there to notice if their prisoner kept escaping, she didn't really have a choice.

The walk back to the Broken Forest was awful. Once the pangolin realized he was being taken somewhere, he started asking questions.

"Where are you taking me?" he said, and "Please, please let me go!" and "If you let me go I won't tell anyone about this," and "Oh Great Dragon, save me!" Nimbletail tried to ignore it, but the strain of not letting go, and not being able to give any reassurance or even an apology made the descent from the foothills feel more like walking up a slope in snow as tall as she was.

She was almost glad when they reached Crookedclaw and Brawnshanks. Crookedclaw took the pangolin from her and nodded to Brawnshanks.

"Good," she said. "Perhaps this one will be more forthcoming than our other prisoner."

"You two have done well," said Brawnshanks. "I can see your loss at the Feats was the troop's gain. This pangolin might not look like much, but he holds the future of the kingdom in his claws. You, Strong Arms!" he waved over a pair of monkeys, and Nimbletail started to see that one of them was Quicktail. She stared at the pangolin in Crookedclaw's hands, and then raised her eyebrows at Nimbletail, who managed a thin smile. "Bring fruit for these two!"

Quicktail's expression cleared and she beamed at Nimbletail before she and her fellow Strong Arm scurried away. It was almost painful for Nimbletail to watch, as she could almost hear her sister's voice in her head—*oh, you've done something good for the troop! I'll get you the best fruit!*

"Thank you, Brawnshanks," said Briskhand, with an unnecessarily deep and elaborate bow. "We live to serve the troop."

Crawler, Nimbletail thought, trying not to let her smile slip.

"Yes," said Brawnshanks dryly. "You do."

Then he left with Crookedclaw and the pangolin, thank the Dragon. Quicktail and the other Strong Arm brought handfuls of ripe and juicy ginkgo fruits and persimmons, and then scurried off to their other duties, leaving her alone with Briskhand.

He made a whooping sound and tucked right in, stuffing a persimmon into his face. But Nimbletail wasn't hungry.

She had just kidnapped a free creature, carried him far from his family, and handed him over to Brawnshanks and Crookedclaw, who wouldn't hesitate to kill him if it served their awful plans. She did that, and all it took was the suggestion that something *might* happen to Quicktail if she didn't.

Anger burned in her heart, like the nutshell on the lava

river, bursting into flame in one bright sizzling moment. She smacked the fruit out of Briskhand's grasp, and when it fell onto the floor, she stomped on it.

"What are you doing?" Briskhand snarled.

Nimbletail didn't answer. She just turned on her heel and stormed away.

What am I doing? Nothing of any use, she thought. *I have to change that. Tonight.*

The tunnels were almost pitch black during the night, so Nimbletail was very glad of the full moon blazing overhead. By the time she'd fumbled her way across the cavern floor to the tunnel entrance the thin shafts of pale moonlight that filtered down into the prison pit seemed almost as bright as daylight.

She had to wait much longer this time, peering through the crack in the wall, for the Strong Arm guard to leave. To Nimbletail's relief, it wasn't Quicktail on duty. She wondered if her sister had been given this job yet, or if Brawnshanks was saving it for his more senior Strong Arms, the ones he knew he could trust with the worst parts of his schemes.

Eventually the guard did leave, yawning hugely. Nimbletail suspected she was sneaking off for an unauthorized nap. She crept into the chamber, suppressing a yawn of her own, and sniffed and listened around at the tunnel entrances to make sure she could whisper to the pangolins without being heard. Finally, distantly, she caught the sound of snoring.

She crept up to the edge of the pit and looked down. The two pangolins were there at the bottom, long, pointy shadows just barely standing out against the darkness.

"It hurts," said one—the younger male, the one Nimbletail had brought. She caught her breath. What had Brawnshanks done to him?

"Hush," said the other. "It's all right, Spiral Moon. If we're very careful it won't hurt."

"But it will," said Spiral Moon, his voice shaking. "The rock fell, and we couldn't get out of the way. . . ."

Nimbletail frowned. She couldn't see a fallen rock in the pit with them at all. What were the pangolins talking about?

"Hello?" she whispered.

The pangolins gasped, and Spiral Moon rolled back into a ball. The other one looked up at Nimbletail, defiance glinting in her eyes. "You again? What do you want now?"

"I want to help you, like I said," Nimbletail said.

"Not interested!" said the pangolin.

"Curling Star," said Spiral Moon, "that's the monkey that kidnapped me!"

"I'm so sorry," said Nimbletail. "I didn't have a choice, I swear."

"More monkey tricks," said the pangolin called Curling Star. "Well, we're not listening. You've done enough damage already."

"You said you were hurt," Nimbletail said, desperate to find some way to show them that she was on their side, before the

Strong Arm heard them and woke up from her nap. "Maybe I can help you?"

"Go away!"

Nimbletail sighed. Perhaps if she came back with food, she could bribe them into believing her? But if they'd only trust her, she might be able to sneak them out right now. . . .

As she stepped back from the edge of the pit she felt a crack under her hand. A rock at the edge of the pit shifted and tilted. A scattering of small rocks were dislodged and fell down, pattering against the pangolins' scales.

"It's happening!" Spiral Moon yelped.

Nimbletail grabbed for the wobbly rock. Spiral Moon was right, a little while longer and it would have fallen right out of the side of the pit! It could have crushed a pangolin's tail or even knocked them on the head! She managed to wiggle her fingers underneath the crack in the rock, and heaved with all her might.

"Move back!" she grunted, scrabbling to keep her grip on the rock as it tipped up toward her. The pangolins pressed themselves against the wall of the pit. Nimbletail braced herself and pulled, and the rock turned over on its end until she could rest it safely on the floor of the cavern. She pushed it up against the wall, to be safe, and then looked down at the pangolins. "Are you both all right?"

Spiral Moon had uncurled, and he was staring up at Nimbletail with bright, glistening eyes. "You stopped it!" he said. "It doesn't hurt any more—you stopped it from falling!"

Nimbletail caught her breath, suddenly understanding. *He saw the rock falling, before it fell. He even felt the pain it was going to cause.*

The pangolins can see the future!

"I really do want to help you," Nimbletail said.

"I believe you," said Spiral Moon. Curling Star still looked a little less sure.

"I'm going to get you out of here," Nimbletail said, "but I need to know what Brawnshanks wants with you two. Did he . . . did he ask you to predict something?" she asked. "Like you did with the rock?"

"No," said Spiral Moon, in a small voice. "It wasn't that."

"It's all my fault," said Curling Star. "I told them the Children of the Dragon knew the story. It's my fault they took you."

"But I'm the one who told them," said Spiral Moon. "I wasn't supposed to tell—no Child of the Dragon has ever told the story to an outsider! But he said he would block up the vents, leave my family with no connection to the Dragon, so . . . I told him everything. I should have been stronger. . . ."

"What was the story?" Nimbletail asked.

"About how the Great Dragon came to be," said Curling Star.

Nimbletail stared into the darkness, her jaw dropping and a nervous prickling sensation running up and down her arms. She'd never heard of such a thing. It had never occurred to her that there was ever a time *before* the Great Dragon.

"Can you tell me?" Nimbletail said. "I know you shouldn't, but . . ."

"It's all right. I'll tell you—if you promise you'll use it to stop Brawnshanks," said Spiral Moon.

"I promise I'll do everything I can," said Nimbletail.

"Well . . ." Spiral Moon took a deep breath. "Once, when the kingdom was new, there wasn't a Great Dragon. There were *two* Dragons, and they ruled over the day and night. The Light Dragon and the Dark Dragon were siblings, and enemies, and the best of friends, all at the same time. They roamed the kingdom, free and wild. And the First Monkey lived in the kingdom too, and she was just as free as the Dragons, but she didn't like them. She thought they had too much power. So she plotted to destroy them."

Nimbletail frowned. It stung, like a splinter digging surprisingly deep into a fingertip, to hear that Brawnshanks had more in common with the First Monkey than she did.

"She knew that the Dragons had a special tie to the pangolins," Spiral Moon went on. "So she put a group of pangolins in terrible danger. She took them down to the fiery heart of the kingdom, and when the Dragons rushed in to save them . . . she thought they would fight each other and destroy themselves. But instead, down in the darkness, they united to save their Children. What emerged was the Great Dragon—one, and whole, and more powerful than the First Monkey could have imagined."

Nimbletail shuddered a little as silence fell in the chamber.

"Did Brawnshanks say why he needed to know the story?" she asked Spiral Moon, rubbing her forehead in puzzlement.

It's just a story—even if it's really true, how does the creation of the Dragon help him?

"I don't know," said Spiral Moon. "But I know he is a bad monkey. Whatever he's planning, it can only be bad, for us and for the Great Dragon itself! You have to—"

"Shh!" Nimbletail hissed.

She'd heard a noise.

"Strikepaw! Get up, you useless lump!" said a horribly familiar voice. It was Crookedclaw.

"I have to go; I'll do what I can!" she whispered to the pangolins, and then as quick as she could move without making any noise, she slipped out the way she had come and pressed her eye to the crack in the wall once more.

Crookedclaw entered, with the Strong Arm, Strikepaw, trailing after her, looking embarrassed. And behind them was Briskhand, with Jitterpaws . . . and two more pangolins. They were rolling them along the ground like squeaking, frightened stones. The monkeys shoved them down into the pit, and Nimbletail winced as she heard the gasps and cries of Spiral Moon and Curling Tail down below.

"Good," said Crookedclaw. "Four is a good start—but Brawnshanks wants more. As many as you can find."

Nimbletail backed away quietly, and padded into the deep darkness of the Feat cavern, stopping to lean against the black wall of the cave and let this sink in.

He's gathering pangolins. Not for their information—he has that. He wants to gather as many pangolins as he can . . .

Spiral Moon's words sat in Nimbletail's heart, like ice.

She put a group of pangolins in terrible danger. She took them down to the fiery heart of the kingdom.

That was why Brawnshanks had brought them to this place. The lava beneath the Broken Forest was the fiery heart of the kingdom. The Great Dragon was made in the dark, lured there by the kidnapping of the pangolins, and Brawnshanks must be intending to do the same again.

He must believe that however the Dragon was made . . . it could be unmade. He's planning to split the Dragon in two.

He hopes to destroy it. And I'm the only one who can stop him!

CHAPTER SIXTEEN

LEAF SAT ON A grassy slope, chewing on the last of the thin stick of bamboo she'd had for the Feast of Golden Light as the dawn broke over the Northern Forest. All around her, red pandas were sitting, talking in low voices or grabbing quick naps while they could. Leaf felt envious of the ones who'd managed to sleep. She'd rested for long enough to observe the feasts, but she hadn't properly slept in almost a day—she'd been walking for a long time, and she was beginning to feel it. Her paw pads ached, and whenever she blinked there was a fraction of a moment when she thought her eyes might simply stay closed.

But she couldn't stop. Not yet. Not here. She had to find the place where the red pandas would be safe, and she couldn't leave them alone until she was sure.

Will I know it when I see it? Leaf wondered. *Will there just be a time when we go far enough that the fire can't get to them?*

How can I know when the fire is coming?

Nothing catastrophic had happened to the Great Dragon yet, despite the pangolins' warnings about the skull hill. Even though she'd seen the fire too, she had to face the fact that there was certainly no fire yet, or else it wasn't where the pangolins had said it would be.

They had walked all night, and not a sniff of smoke or a distant crackle had reached them. The rising sun glinted from the golden ginkgo trees, as whole and unburnt as they'd been when they had set off.

"We should move on," she said, after she'd given the red pandas the longest break she could.

A chorus of grunts and grumbles greeted this news.

"Can't we go home?" said Jumper Climbing Far, squinting down the hill. "I don't see any fire!"

"Shush," said Seeker Climbing Far, Dasher's mother. "We need to trust the Dragon Speaker. I'm sure it's not much farther."

Leaf smiled at her. *I hope you're right,* she thought.

Dasher hurried over to Leaf's side as the pandas got to their paws and nudged their sleeping families awake, and together they started to gather them and lead them on up the slope. Leaf tried to think. If there was a fire in the Slenderwood, how far would it spread, and which way? She stood at the top of the slope for a moment, feeling the wind in her fur. It was blowing south, so if they just went a little farther north, and made sure they had a good lookout on watch for any smoke, then the red pandas would be safe. She hoped.

"Still don't get it," muttered one of them, from behind Leaf. "Dasher said we're doing this because of *pangolins?*"

"They read our fortune," said another. "In an anthill."

"So Leaf made us walk all night because a bunch of pangolins saw some ants move in a funny way?"

Leaf glanced back and saw that it was Thumper Digging Deep, questioning his sister Chomper. Chomper shook her head.

"But Leaf had a vision of her own. That's *two* warnings from the Great Dragon! You can't question that," she said.

"That's right!" said Hopper Leaping High, who was walking behind the two of them with her tail swishing. "Have either of *you* met the Great Dragon? If the Speaker *and* the pangolins say there's danger, we have to believe them."

Leaf smiled to herself, grateful to Hopper for sticking up for her decisions. Her words stuck with her as they walked. Wasn't it strange that the Dragon had sent the same message to the pangolins and to her? What did that mean?

Maybe . . . it was so that I would believe the pangolins, when they arrived, she thought. *I might have ignored them otherwise! After all, I'd just got back from what seemed like a wild goose chase up the mountain and back again.*

All the more reason to get the red pandas to safety, then.

"There's a lot of dawdling back there," said Dasher, also

looking over his shoulder at the last handful of red pandas as they made their way up the slope. "I'll go and try to hurry them up."

He scampered off, and Leaf waited for a moment, before turning to carry on the journey. She scanned the land around her, and finally she thought she spotted what she was looking for—a patch of trees on a steep rocky hillside, separated from the rest of the forest by an open space. No fire should be able to leap to those trees.

"Leaf!" She looked back as she heard Dasher's voice calling out from behind. He was scampering up the slope, running anxious circles around the red pandas who were bringing up the rear, looking back all the time. "Something's not right," he said as they all drew closer.

"What is it?" she asked, peering back down the slope. She couldn't see any smoke, or anything else for that matter, apart from grass and rock and trees and the long morning shadows.

"We're being followed," said Hunter Leaping High. "I scented something—but I don't know what it was."

"It's just like when we were heading for the mountain," said Dancer Leaping High. "And we knew that tiger was after us, but we didn't see any sign of it until . . ." She trailed off, but turned on the spot as if she thought she would see whatever it was if she just kept looking. No creature needed to finish her sentence for her—all of them remembered the awful sight of Scratcher Climbing Far's half-devoured body.

"I don't think it's a tiger," said Leaf. "I've only ever seen one tiger in the kingdom, and . . ." she trailed off. Shadowhunter the tiger, the chosen Watcher of the last true Dragon Speaker, was dead.

He was a predator, and he could be terrifying. He never apologized for his appetite. But he was also wise, and strong, and he cared about the kingdom and the Dragon Speakers.

He cared so much that he'd thrown himself into the great pit at the heart of the Dragon Mountain, taking Dusk Deepwood down with him, to protect Leaf and her siblings. She sometimes wished he was still around to advise her, even though she knew that would mean putting some creature somewhere in terrible danger.

"Let's just keep going," Dasher said. "The sooner we find somewhere safe to settle, the better."

The Leaping Highs agreed, but they still seemed very jumpy as they followed the others, looking back down the slope, and then sometimes up at the sky, as if they weren't sure whether the danger they sensed was coming from the trees or out of the clouds. Leaf suspected they were more worried than they were letting on—they certainly seemed unsettled, as if they half expected a fire to come out of nowhere.

The closer they drew to the rocky slope with the isolated trees that Leaf had noticed before, the more certain she was that it was the best place for them to be. Bamboo grew in scattered clumps from between the rocks, so there would be something for them to eat right away, and for however long they ended up staying here. And the clump of trees she'd seen from far away turned out to be three huge trees, with spreading branches, each one of which seemed to lean against and twine through the others, forming a sprawling but connected colony of branches and roots.

"Triplets!" Dasher exclaimed, as he looked up and saw the three trees. "They must represent the Dragon Speakers! Do you think this is it?"

"I think so," said Leaf.

Some of the red pandas began to climb into the trees, sniffing approvingly at their new home, while others investigated the bamboo, pulling down leaves and chewing thoughtfully.

"It's a good place," said Seeker, draping her tail comfortingly between Leaf's paws. "Thank you. Now you should rest! You look exhausted."

"I could do with a nap," Leaf admitted. "I almost feel as if it's starting to get dark already!" She blinked a couple of times, trying to clear her eyes. All the shadows suddenly seemed deeper, like the long black shadows of late afternoon.

"Leaf . . . ?" said Dasher. "I think it *is* getting darker."

"What?" Leaf frowned at Dasher, and then looked up into the sky. It was blue and clear, although there was something that looked like a deep gray storm cloud on the horizon.

But . . .

"I think there's something . . ." Leaf broke off. It sounded so bizarre, and she couldn't be sure—it seemed harder than usual to look at the sun, let alone be sure there was something *wrong* with it. And yet that was the feeling.

She hoped that the strange quality of the light would subside, but it didn't. One by one, the red pandas stopped their chatter and their exploration of the trees, and the ones who were still awake turned to each other, to the sky, and to Leaf, as the day grew unmistakably dimmer.

"What's happening?" asked Seeker. "It's not even High Sun yet, and there's no clouds above us! So how can it be getting dark?"

Leaf took a deep breath.

"It's the Dark Sun. It's here," she said.

Dasher started, and looked at her. The light was so strange now, his red fur looked washed out and silvery, but the shadows were so sharp she could almost pick out each individual hair on his head. "What does it mean?"

"I don't know," said Leaf. "But I think it's something terrible."

She looked around her, desperate for a sign, anything *other* than the strange gloom descending over the kingdom, to tell her what she needed to *do*. There was nothing.

"I'm going up to the top, I have to see what's happening," she garbled, and took off at a scrambling run up over the rocks. She was comforted, a little, by the sound of Dasher's paws on the slope right behind her.

At the top of the hill, she gasped, blinking again as she looked north toward the White Spine Mountains. The snowy caps were a jagged patchwork of glowing white so bright it made Leaf turn her head away and shadows so sharp and dark that she couldn't see anything within them. And as she turned to take in the rest of the kingdom, it was the same everywhere—violent greens and golds, sparkling rocks and streams, and black shadows in between them. The whole world was shifting and changing, and she didn't understand.

She tried, once more, to look up. She took a single, quick glance up at the sun, and then had to look away. It was brighter than it should be, and yet the world was darker—and when Leaf closed her eyes, a swirling afterimage danced in front of her—but the shape of it wasn't right. Instead of a perfect circle, it was an odd egg shape, like the moon when it was a few days away from being full.

"Something is wrong with the sun!" she said. "The Dark Sun is rising. And I have no idea what to do." She sat down, closed her eyes, and focused on the strange afterimage. "Great Dragon, help me. . . ."

The afterimage in her mind swirled dizzily, but instead of slowly fading, it suddenly seemed to glow even brighter, changing shape before her shut eyes, until she found herself staring once more at the black branch wreathed in white fire. It was closer now, right in front of her, and on the branch there was a single, blazing leaf.

Is that . . . me?

The fire almost seemed to be spreading from the *leaf,* not the branch, leaping to the leaves of the trees all around, consuming the forest in moments. . . .

A scream tore through the air, and Leaf's eyes snapped open.

"Mother!" Dasher gasped, and set off back down the slope

at a skidding run. Leaf tried to focus on the trees, but the strange light and shadow and the mass of panicking red pandas blocked her view for a moment—and then she saw the lithe white shapes, and heard another red panda's scream cut off with a horrible gargle. The hillside echoed with cries and shouts, panic and horror.

The red pandas were under attack.

I didn't save them at all. I brought them into terrible danger!

CHAPTER SEVENTEEN

"WHAT IS IT? WHAT'S happening?"

Ghost sat beneath a tree in the Northern Forest, listening to a pair of squirrels chittering in the branches above, and wondering exactly the same thing. A shudder ran through him as he looked out at the Bamboo Kingdom, bathed in strange and frightening light.

The Dark Sun. It had to be. This was Leaf's message from the Great Dragon coming true. She'd failed to stop it. Was she even supposed to stop it?

We never worked out what it meant. What if . . . what if it's me?

He'd left his mountains, given away his Dragon Speaker stone, been chased away by the other pandas, been rejected by Rain. What if this was the Dragon's way of telling the kingdom that there had been a disaster, that there were just two

Dragon Speakers now?

But his problems weren't the only ones in the Kingdom, he knew that well enough.

What if it's not me—but Pebble? What if his murder has made this happen?

What's Rain doing? How are the Prosperhill pandas reacting?

There was no point wondering about it. He couldn't go back there.

What could he do, if the world might be ending? He had to head toward to the mountains and find Shiver. She had the stone. And if the sun was falling from the sky, or the kingdom was to be plunged into eternal darkness . . . then at least they could face it together.

He didn't think it *really* helped to have leaves and branches between him and the strange sky, but it was still oddly hard to leave the shelter of the tree. He stepped out into the bizarre light, flinching a little as he felt the sun on his fur.

The air was turning oddly cold.

Is something even worse on the way?

He made his way north, sticking to the valleys and crevices between the hillsides whenever he could. He wasn't sure why—down here in the shadows, the chill was much harsher. But something made him want to stay away from the peaks of the rolling hills, as if being exposed to the strange sky would be dangerous.

He hoped that Shiver had come this way too, or at least that they would meet up somewhere in the mountains. Perhaps she would be somehow protected from all this, because she had the Dragon Speaker's stone? Perhaps she would be in even *more* danger, if the Dark Sun was somehow focused on the Speakers? Possibilities kept spinning around his head as he passed between the trees and along the bed of a dried-up stream. They were like wisps of cloud, each one thin and insubstantial. The fact was, he had no idea what was happening, and that was the most frightening thing of all. . . .

Until he heard the screams of terror up ahead.

He startled and came to a stop. They were coming from a hillside nearby, probably the other side of the hill he was walking in the shadow of right now. He skidded around on the dry streambed and broke into a run, scrambling up over rocks and onto the hill, running on a steep slope dotted with a few thin patches of bamboo.

The awful scene emerged gradually as he circled the hillside—the tops of trees, bowing branches crowded with fearful, crying red pandas. They clung to every branch, some covering their eyes with their fluffy paws, others growling down at the ground, tails puffed with desperate anger. There were yowling noises and yelps of pain.

And then he saw what was happening on the ground: two snow leopards were circling the trees, and a panda was desperately trying to face off with them, standing over the bleeding body of a red panda. Two more bodies lay nearby, red fur scattered across the rocks.

It was Brisk and Sleet killing the red pandas, and Leaf

standing between them and the trees, her legs visibly shaking. Horror made Ghost's own legs feel heavy, and he stumbled clumsily and tripped over a rock, unable to take his eyes from the awful scene in front of him.

"Get away!" Leaf yelled. "I'll kill you!"

The leopards laughed at her.

Ghost began to growl, deep in his throat, building to a roar so loud it echoed off the hillside. Brisk and Sleet both looked up, and their mocking expressions turned to anger. Ghost charged, bowling right toward Brisk's chest. Leaf gasped, and then she sprang too, running at Sleet with her claws bared. Ghost landed on top of Brisk instead of running into her, and he sank his teeth into Brisk's shoulder. But then he heard Leaf yelp again, and as he was turning to look he felt Sleet's paws come down on top of him, rolling him off his sister. He landed on his back and slid a few paw steps down the rocky slope.

Looking up, he saw the frightened eyes of the red pandas staring at him.

He rolled and scrambled back to his paws. Leaf was panting, bleeding from a tear across her muzzle, but still trying to swipe at Sleet. She seized him by the tail, her tough panda jaws biting down hard, and Sleet yowled in pain. Brisk was advancing, but Ghost rolled out of the way of her claws and then head-butted her hard in the shoulder where blood was seeping through her thick fur, making her reel and yelp.

"You should never have come down from the mountain,"

Ghost snarled, and grabbed Brisk by the scruff and threw her over onto her back.

"This . . . isn't like that scrap at the river," Brisk gasped, winded by the fall onto the rocks. "We're not fighting for show this time! Kill her, Sleet!"

Ghost looked around, just in time to see Sleet turning on Leaf, still tethered to her by the tail, rearing up with both paws raised to bring them down on Leaf's face. Ghost charged, got between them and swiped at Sleet's exposed belly, drawing blood and sending him flying.

"The cubs Born of Winter should have defeated you many seasons ago," Ghost snarled. "We should have thrown you into the Endless Maw when you first tried to hurt us!"

"We're not the ones who almost fell to our deaths at the Maw," spat Sleet. "Let *go!*" He tugged at his tail, and Leaf glanced at Ghost. He nodded.

"Give him the chance to run," he told her. "Anyway, at least I was brave enough to *try* to jump the Maw."

"I'm sure your dead mother is very proud of you," Brisk sneered. "Maybe you could go to the bottom of the Maw and ask her."

Ghost felt as if Brisk's teeth had closed over his heart. He bunched his muscles to spring at her, but realized Sleet was watching him, crouching with wide eyes as if he was going to pounce the moment he moved. He froze, bracing against the rocks.

"If you want to go on with your sorry lives," he said, "leave this place and go far away from the Bamboo Kingdom. Otherwise, my sister and I will kill you for what you've done."

"Go on, Leaf!" cried one of the red pandas. "Get them!"

A hail of small stones suddenly pelted down on top of Sleet, and Ghost looked up, afraid that this was part of the darkening sky, that the Dark Sun was throwing out hailstones made of actual stone—but it was the red pandas. A few of them had climbed out to the very edge of the branches with mouths full of stones and were dropping them down on the leopards' heads. Sleet recoiled, stumbled, and hissed up at the red pandas.

"We'll see you again," he snarled at Ghost. "We're not finished with you yet."

"You'll wish you never left your mother's den, freak," spat Brisk.

Ghost kept his eyes on them as they backed off, watching carefully for any sign that they might charge again. He kept watching as they walked away, until they had vanished out of sight, and then he turned to look at Leaf.

She was nuzzling at the bodies of the red pandas. There were three of them, all dead, and as Ghost watched another one clambered out of the tree on three good legs, one leg dragging uselessly behind her.

"Mother!" cried the red panda Dasher, running over to the wounded one. He rubbed his face against hers and she sat down heavily, and then flopped onto her side, breathing hard.

"R-roller?" said another red panda. She was staring at the

body of the one Leaf was tending to, her eyes wide.

"I'm sorry, Hopper," Leaf said. "He's gone."

The red panda called Hopper burst into a keening wail and laid down beside the body of Roller. More red pandas emerged from the trees and ran to their fallen friends, crying their names. And above them, the strange light had hardly changed—the sun seemed even more painfully bright, even as the shadows grew darker and the air felt more like twilight than the middle of the day.

Leaf looked up at Ghost. She seemed exhausted.

"The Dark Sun is here," she said. "The Dragon sent it to warn me . . . it sent the pangolins, but there was no fire, and now I've led them here and this is all my fault. I didn't listen, and the Dark Sun is here and . . ."

Ghost ran up to her and gently licked her wounds, nudging her to sit down on a flat rock.

"I don't understand," Ghost said. "I don't know what's going on—but I know this isn't your fault. If anything, it's mine. Brisk and Sleet only came this far south to mess with me."

"What do you mean?" Leaf asked. "Ghost, I'm glad you were here, but—but what are you doing here? I went to look for you in the far north, and you weren't there . . . the animals seemed terrified of you, they said you'd left. And then I went to the Egg Rocks at the full moon, like we agreed, and you weren't there, and Rain didn't turn up either. I've got so much I've needed your help with and now the Dark Sun is *here* and it's too late . . . what do you mean, it's your fault?"

Ghost hesitated. Where could he begin?

A chill wind was blowing over the hillside now. The red pandas were gathering up their dead. He looked over the Northern Forest and saw darkness flowing toward them, like the shadow of a huge storm cloud, despite the clear sky.

"Brisk and Sleet are leopards that Shiver and I know from when we were cubs. They hate us. When I got to the mountains, everything was fine for a few days—and then they came. They told me they were going to ruin my life, and they told all the animals I was a predator and they couldn't trust me, and then I caught them talking about going to the Southern Forest to hunt pandas, so I had to go, I had to try to warn Rain . . . but when I got there, they'd already . . ."

He broke off. What was it Brisk had said? *This isn't like that scrap at the river, we're not fighting for show this time.*

"We fought, but it was a trick, just long enough for me to have blood in my fur. I found Rain, but I was too late—Pebble was dead. That was why Rain and I missed the meeting at the full moon. And then Blossom and Ginseng lied and said they'd seen me there earlier and I'd done it, presumably to cover their tracks. . . ."

Leaf's eyes were huge and dark, and she was shaking her head. "Wait, I don't understand," she said. "So who did kill him? Blossom and Ginseng? Or the leopards?"

"I—I don't . . ." Ghost felt dizzy just trying to tell the story, as if there was a piece missing and he knew it, but he couldn't figure out what it was.

If Brisk and Sleet killed Pebble, why would Blossom and Ginseng try to pin it on Ghost? But if the pandas did it, why would the snow leopards have known to make sure he arrived there bloody? They couldn't be working together . . . could they?

"Poor Pebble," murmured Leaf. "And poor Rain . . ."

"They said I did it," Ghost went on. "And they threw me out—Rain said I wasn't a Dragon Speaker anymore. They tried to take my stone, but I sent Shiver away with it. Leaf . . . I don't know what's happening to the sky, I don't know about any fire. But I need your help. You need to talk to Rain, get her to see that I would never hurt Pebble!"

"You need my help?" said Leaf, and Ghost's heart sank as he heard the chill in her voice. She stood up and backed away from him, shaking her head. "That's right, everybody always needs *my* help. Did you know that the mountain creatures were trekking all the way down to *my* territory to ask for advice, because they couldn't trust you?"

"I—no, but . . ." Ghost began, but Leaf cut him off.

"The pangolins told me to go to the skull hill, that the monkeys were going to destroy the Great Dragon. They weren't there. You weren't there. Nothing was there. I ran all the way. Do *you* know what the monkeys are up to, Ghost? I don't, because *I needed your help!*"

Ghost flinched, guilt and anger growing side by side. "I want to help you, but I told you, I thought the leopards were going to murder half the Prosperhill! I don't know why they're so obsessed with bringing me down, but I had to stop them!"

"But you failed to," Leaf said. She glanced up at the sky once more. "I can't talk to Rain for you. I need to hear her side of the story first. Maybe the Dark Sun isn't just a warning to me...."

"Are you saying you think I killed Pebble?" Ghost snapped.

"I'm saying maybe Rain's right, and you're not cut out to be the holder of that stone," Leaf snarled back.

"I did my best! I ran all night, down from the mountains, to try to save the Prosperhill pandas! The Dragon never said a word, I had to find out about the danger all on my own...." Ghost broke off. He was just proving Leaf's point, but he knew in his heart she was wrong. He had to find Shiver and get his stone back.... "You normal pandas ... you'll never accept me. Even my own sisters. But remember that I'm not the one who put my friends in danger running from a fire that didn't even happen," he snarled.

Leaf startled, and her cold demeanor froze over. "Leave me alone, Ghost," she said.

"I'm going," said Ghost. "Good luck figuring out how to bring the sun back; I'm sure you and Rain will do fine all by yourselves."

And he turned and walked away, heading north and not looking back.

CHAPTER EIGHTEEN

IT'S HAPPENING.

Nimbletail was marching through the Broken Forest beside Crookedclaw. In front of them walked a group of other monkeys, each one either carrying a curled-up pangolin in their arms or prodding one to run along the ground in front of them with a stick, and up above, the sun was blazing madly while the light all around them somehow grew dimmer and dimmer. The shadows of the jagged, broken trees cut across their path, making the pale earth look as if it had split open.

I thought I'd have more time! Nimbletail thought desperately. She thought she'd have a few days, or even longer, to find out Brawnshanks's plans and find a way to stop him—but whatever it was, it had already begun.

The pangolins were coiled in trembling bundles or trudging along, none of them fighting their captors—but they weren't quiet, either.

"The Dark Sun," said one, in a singsong voice, looking up at the sky.

"The Dark Sun!" echoed several more, including muffled voices from within the curled shapes being carried by the Strong Arms. "It has come!"

"The sun will die," said another. "And be reborn!"

"Shut up, you lot," said Crookedclaw, though she didn't sound as worried as Nimbletail felt—or as several of the other monkeys looked—at the idea that the sun might be *dying*.

What did she know that they didn't?

"Hurry," Crookedclaw added, prodding a dawdling monkey in the back with a long finger. "We don't have much time."

I could attack her now, Nimbletail thought. *Bring her down, and I bet a lot of Brawnshanks's plans crumble with her.*

But if she didn't kill me, the other monkeys would. They might hurt the pangolins, and even if they all got away, there are more under the ground. . . .

It wasn't the right move, but Nimbletail felt more and more desperate as they approached the tunnel entrance and began to vanish inside.

If not that, what? If not now, when? Great Dragon, I don't know what to do. . . .

It was almost a relief to get underground, out of sight of the strange sky.

* * *

Crookedtail was leading them to the prison pit, of that much Nimbletail was certain—they would get there via the tunnel entrance she'd seen the Strong Arms going in and out through, and presumably then the pangolins would be thrown in with the others.

But when they approached, she heard voices, pangolin and monkey mixed together, up ahead.

"Briskhand, are they all there?" Crookedclaw called down the tunnel. Their group drew closer, and Nimbletail frowned as she saw a turn in the tunnel up ahead where it split into two paths. Briskhand and another group, much like theirs, was shepherding a handful of pangolins out of the prison side on the left, and into the turning on the right.

"All of them," said Briskhand, with insufferable smugness.

"Then down we go, and quickly," said Crookedclaw. "And keep an eye on the creatures. We need them all, and if you lose one, Brawnshanks will have your head."

Why? Why do they need so many? Nimbletail thought frantically, as their group followed down the right-hand path, behind the crowd of nervously chattering pangolins.

It was a steep descent, and for a time it was pitch black. Nimbletail went carefully, listening to the small sounds of others occasionally losing their footing or stepping too hard on a jagged part of the rock. And then she saw a glow at the bottom of the tunnel, as it evened out to a shallower slope. It was a horribly familiar bright orange light, and sure enough, as soon as they stepped out of the tunnel she felt her hair curling with the heat of the lava river.

It took a moment of blinking in the uncomfortable dry heat before Nimbletail realized where they were. It was the very same chamber where the Third Feat had taken place, but the steep tunnel had taken them down to a lower ledge, closer to the fire. The heat was almost unbearable.

Brawnshanks was sitting on the ledge, close to the lava, his eyes half-closed as he contemplated the awful brightness of it. The Strong Arms and Crookedclaw's spies were gathering the pangolins together in one big, trembling group.

"The Dark Sun!" squeaked one, in a small voice, and Briskhand smacked it casually on the head.

A few chuckles made Nimbletail look up. She saw that there were monkeys on the upper level, crowded onto the ledges that had formed the beginning and end of the Feat, and some brave ones sitting on the paths that clung to the walls too. They were looking down with expectant faces. She saw Quicktail up there, with some of the Strong Arms guiding monkeys to move along the walls to get a better look. Swingtail was there too. She couldn't see Goldback or Flicktail. Quicktail looked down and saw Nimbletail, and waved, with an excited grin. Nimbletail didn't wave back.

Does she really think this is a good idea? she thought gloomily. *She's only been a Strong Arm for a few days—is it that quick for the brain rot to sink in?*

"My fellow monkeys," Brawnshanks said, holding up his arms. His voice had a strange quality in this boiling cavern.

It seemed louder, even though he wasn't shouting. "This is a very special place. This is where everything has been leading us. Every fight, every move we've made against the pandas and their tyranny, has been so that we would control this very place. This is the deal we made with Dusk Deepwood. This is why I've called you all here, from all corners of the kingdom—a gathering of monkeys like there has never been before!"

Many of the monkeys whooped and hollered at this. Nimbletail winced. She started looking around the cave, wondering if there were other ways into this space that she hadn't seen before. She saw several—this place was actually a nexus of tunnel entrances, some leading from the ledge where she was standing now, and a few that didn't even have ledges, but opened onto sheer rock walls where anyone who emerged from them would fall directly into the lava.

"This is the place where the Great Dragon was created," said Brawnshanks. "And this is where it will be destroyed! Its power will pass to us, and the age of the pandas will end! Monkeys will rule the Bamboo Kingdom, at last!"

Cheering resounded around the chamber. Nimbletail looked up, hoping that she might finally see Quicktail realize that this was a terrible, dangerous plan. . . . But though a few of the monkey faces she saw were drawn in uncertainty or surprise, there was no hesitation on Quicktail's. She clapped and whooped along with Brawnshanks's most fervent supporters.

"Drive them toward the fire!" Crookedclaw said.

Her spies began to force the pangolins forward. Some of

them curled into terrified balls, and the monkeys simply rolled them toward the edge. Nimbletail hesitated for a moment, and then stepped up alongside the others, falling into place behind Curling Star. She had to do something, she *couldn't* just stand and watch. . . .

She bent down, pretending to prod Curling Star in the tail.

"I'm here," she whispered. "Tell the others, when I say run, you run as fast as you can."

"Please," Curling Star replied. "Please, don't let them hurt us. . . ."

They were a single monkey-stride from the edge. Nimbletail tensed. From here if she vaulted the pangolins and shoved Briskhand aside she might be able to get to Brawnshanks. She had to try. If she could surprise him, she could knock him off the edge. . . .

But then gasps filled the chamber, and Brawnshanks held up his hand.

"Stop," Crookedclaw called. The pangolins milled in a horrified crush, trying to back away from the ledge, but the Strong Arms and the spies kept them pinned. From the ledges above her, Nimbletail saw monkeys pointing and heard them call out, "What is that? What's happening?"

The lava river was bubbling and swirling. Bright spurts of boiling stone spat up from its surface, and almost burned the face of one of the monkeys who was leaning over the edge. The black ash that swirled on top of the river began to turn from a slow flow to a spiral shape as the river itself twisted and began to rise. This time, the Strong Arms also took a step back, and pangolins and guards moved together away from the edge.

"The Dragon is angry," said Curling Star. "It knows they've taken the Children of the Dragon. It's coming to take them back!"

"Can we stop it?" Nimbletail whispered.

"The Dark Sun rises," said Spiral Moon. "The Dragon is coming!"

The river swirled faster, and the center of the swirl began to sink even as the rest was still rising—a whirlpool of molten rock with a deep, dark hole at its center. A roar reverberated around the cavern, and the monkeys clutched each other and hooted in fear and excitement. The sound was like the roar of a furious creature, and like rock being torn asunder, and like thunder rolling, all at once.

Brawnshanks's eyes were wide and full of the bright reflection of the swirling lava, as smoke began to pour from the center of the whirlpool, but it didn't disperse and fill the cavern—it flowed into the huge shape of a creature. A wide head, with long whiskers, and a coal-black body. Red lightning flashed through the smoke, and when it passed Nimbletail she could see scales. Two enormous claws pulled up out of the whirlpool and slapped down onto the surface of the lava, sending up splashes of rock.

It turned its head to the ledge and opened up its eyes. They were made of flame, burning deep inside the head.

Nimbletail reeled, and almost fell to the ground.

The Great Dragon. It was real—it was here, right in front of her.

And it was in terrible danger.

For a moment, there was almost silence in the cavern, as the monkeys stared and gibbered to each other, and the pangolins whimpered. Brawnshanks stood and looked up, directly into the Dragon's eyes, and Nimbletail saw a flicker of terror in his face. Then he grinned.

"Now!" cried Brawnshanks. "Take them! Split them up!"

"You," Crookedclaw said, pointing to Briskhand, "take one group that way. You," she pointed to the monkey standing beside Nimbletail, "that way. Go!"

The monkeys began to shove the pangolins into one of two groups, and Nimbletail understood.

He wants to split the Dragon by making it chase both sets of pangolins at once.

There was nothing she could do for the pangolins who Briskhand was shoving into the tunnel on the other side of the ledge. But if she could at least save *some* of them . . .

The Dragon roared again, and fire licked over their heads. The monkeys ducked, covering their faces as smoke and ash swirled through the air.

"Get them out of here!" yelled Crookedclaw again.

"Now, Curling Star!" Nimbletail hissed. "Follow me!"

She backed away, while chaos and smoke filled the chamber, and so did the Dragon's roars and the screams of the monkeys who suddenly found themselves at head-height with it. She saw Curling Star nudge another pangolin, who nudged a third, and as she reached the tunnel they'd come down she saw that a small group of them had split off, hurrying on their stubby back legs.

She turned and ran, into the tunnel, and began to climb the steep rocky slope. She could hear the sound of pangolins climbing behind her, and hoped they weren't having trouble with keeping a grip on the rough rocks, but after no time at all they were climbing through pitch darkness, and even if she'd wanted to stop, she couldn't see how many pangolins were with her.

They got to the top of the slope and kept on running, Nimbletail fumbling her way through the darkness to make sure she'd taken the fork in the tunnel that would lead them up to the surface, instead of back to the prison cave, and finally they burst, panting, out from underground and into the open air.

Nimbletail staggered to a stop, a little way from the mouth of the tunnel, and stared around in horror.

It was dark, as dark as if it was the middle of the night. She peered up at where the sun should have been, expecting to find nothing, a blank void. . . .

But there was something there, in place of the sun. A black circle, surrounded by flecks of brilliant, flickering white light. The stars were out, blazing as bright as they would on the clearest night. And even stranger, at the edges of the sky, she could make out a strip of brighter blue, almost as if there was an ordinary day that was happening, but simply not *here*.

She looked down as the pangolins ran past her, out into the forest. It wasn't all of them—only Curling Star and five others had made it out. But Nimbletail's heart swelled to see them scamper off into the trees.

Even if this was the end, if Brawnshanks had succeeded, and he would rule over this kingdom of eternal night, at least she would know she had done everything she could.

Curling Star paused, looking up at the sky, and then turned to Nimbletail.

"I'm sorry," Nimbletail said. "I'm sorry I couldn't stop it!"

"The Dark Sun is here," said the pangolin. "But don't despair. You don't yet know what your actions here have done. All of the Bamboo Kingdom is in darkness, and that darkness will linger . . . but a new day waits on the horizon, thanks to you."

Nimbletail didn't know what to say. She held her hand to her heart, praying that Curling Star was right.

"Now, go, and witness the Dragon's rebirth—someone must tell the Speakers what happened here," Curling Star said. "Hurry!"

Nimbletail nodded, overwhelmed, and turned and ran back into the caverns, scampering down the dark passages, rebounding off walls and skidding on loose earth, until she snuck from the tunnel mouth into the bright lava cavern, and saw . . .

It was like nothing she could have dreamed. It was like a nightmare.

The Dragon was twitching and curling around itself, trying to pull one way and then another, and as it did so, it seemed to shift and split—one moment it had one head, and then two, or more, blurring and changing like the afterimage from looking at the sun. It hurt to watch. Several monkeys clutched their heads or covered their eyes. Brawnshanks and Crookedclaw were both staring at it. Neither of them seemed to have noticed Nimbletail stealing away with the pangolins.

"Yes!" Brawnshanks was shrieking. "It's working! It's . . ."

And then there was a sound like a thousand creatures all taking a deep breath at the same time, and the Great Dragon split apart, as neatly as a ripe nut coming free from its shell.

One of the Dragons blazed, casting shifting light across the chamber. Nimbletail could hardly look at it—it flowed like the lava river, but it shone pale and brilliant like the light of the stars, or sunlight on snow, and its eyes were like two suns.

The next was darkness—not the black coal darkness of the smoke that had made up its body earlier, but the absolute absence of light, a shadow that cast itself across the walls of the cave. No matter how she tried, Nimbletail couldn't make out eyes or scales or claws, unless they were silhouetted against its light sibling.

The two dragons swirled around each other, like fish caught in the rapids of the river. Nimbletail's heart hurt as she saw that they seemed much smaller than the Great Dragon had been.

"Now!" shrieked Brawnshanks. "Release the power of the Great Dragon to me! I have defeated you!"

"Wait," Crookedclaw said. "What is *that?*"

She pointed across the lava, and the monkeys gasped.

There was a third dragon.

It was made of shifting light and darkness, sometimes almost invisible, other times shining with color, like the faint rainbows that shimmered across the sky after a storm. One moment it seemed to be made of water, another moment it looked like crystal. For a brief heartbeat it turned its eyes on Nimbletail, and she saw her own reflection looking back, as if she was looking into two still pools in black rock.

The third dragon seemed to hypnotize all the monkeys—even Brawnshanks and Crookedclaw were silent, eyes wide and jaws slack.

Then the third dragon joined the light and dark. Together they swirled faster and faster, until they flew apart, tails whipping behind them. They vanished into the mouths of the tunnels and were gone.

The shifting light went out, and all that was left was the dull glow of the lava as it slurped back into its ordinary form.

"No!" Brawnshanks screamed. "Crookedclaw! What happened? It was supposed to be destroyed!" He turned to her and shoved her hard, not in the direction of the lava, but close enough that the other monkeys gasped, and Nimbletail thought she caught Crookedclaw giving Brawnshanks a furious glare and taking a deep breath.

"Perhaps someone interfered with the ceremony," she said. "I will find out who, and have them lowered feet first into the lava. And perhaps they did us a favor, in the end. After all, three dragons may be even weaker than two."

Brawnshanks didn't look convinced, but he didn't lash out at her again. He turned to the assembled monkeys and threw his hands into the air.

"Now, my monkeys, the great hunt begins! The Dragons are vulnerable! They have great power, but they *can* be destroyed. We will hunt them down and obliterate them!"

Some monkeys cheered. Some ran from the chamber at once, hooting about the chase. A few looked simply too shocked to move and sat there staring into the lava, whimpering to themselves. Nimbletail searched the crowd for Quicktail, and found her ushering the other monkeys back to the tunnels, guiding the ones who seemed too startled to look where they were going. For almost the first time in their lives, Nimbletail couldn't read her expression.

"Let's go!" said one of the Strong Arms near Nimbletail. She forced a whoop, and seized the opportunity to escape from that place. She clambered back up the steep tunnel and staggered outside . . . into a patch of bright sunshine.

She tried to peer up at the sun, but it blazed too bright to see, just like it had before, casting the same strange silvery light and sharp shadows. The stars were gone, and the sky was blue—the same blue she'd seen as a line on the horizon as the pangolins escaped.

A new dawn has come, she thought. *Because there was a third group, another way for the dragon to go . . . because some of the pangolins got away. Because of me.*

She didn't know what would happen next, but as she sat down on a rock and watched the strange light lift from the Bamboo Kingdom, she knew that there was hope.

"Perhaps someone interfered with the ceremony," she said. "I will find out who, and have them lowered feet first into the lava. And perhaps they did us a favor, in the end. After all, three dragons may be even weaker than two."

Brawnshanks didn't look convinced, but he didn't lash out at her again. He turned to the assembled monkeys and threw his hands into the air.

"Now, my monkeys, the great hunt begins! The Dragons are vulnerable! They have great power, but they *can* be destroyed. We will hunt them down and obliterate them!"

Some monkeys cheered. Some ran from the chamber at once, hooting about the chase. A few looked simply too shocked to move and sat there staring into the lava, whimpering to themselves. Nimbletail searched the crowd for Quicktail, and found her ushering the other monkeys back to the tunnels, guiding the ones who seemed too startled to look where they were going. For almost the first time in their lives, Nimbletail couldn't read her expression.

"Let's go!" said one of the Strong Arms near Nimbletail. She forced a whoop, and seized the opportunity to escape from that place. She clambered back up the steep tunnel and staggered outside . . . into a patch of bright sunshine.

She tried to peer up at the sun, but it blazed too bright to see, just like it had before, casting the same strange silvery light and sharp shadows. The stars were gone, and the sky was blue—the same blue she'd seen as a line on the horizon as the pangolins escaped.

A new dawn has come, she thought. *Because there was a third group, another way for the dragon to go . . . because some of the pangolins got away. Because of me.*

She didn't know what would happen next, but as she sat down on a rock and watched the strange light lift from the Bamboo Kingdom, she knew that there was hope.

CHAPTER NINETEEN

LEAF WALKED ALONG THE top of the hill, alone, in the darkness. The Dark Sun glowed above, a black orb ringed with sparkling light. The night had fallen so suddenly that the red pandas had run for cover, but Leaf had found she wasn't surprised. Why shouldn't darkness cover the kingdom? She hadn't done anything to prevent it.

The Dragon wasn't trying to warn me about the fire. It was trying to warn me . . . about me.

For the red pandas, she had been as deadly as a raging forest fire. She was the leaf that had brought destruction to them. That was what the Dragon had tried to show her, but she'd been too concerned with what Ghost was doing to see it.

She had to walk. She couldn't make herself stop or sit down. Her paws wanted to keep moving, and she indulged them.

She thought she might walk forever, through the long night. There was light on the horizon, almost like the dawn, but it was wrong—too stark and unmoving, not like Gray Light or Golden Light at all.

"Leaf!" cried a voice. She stopped, and turned. It was Dasher. He was running up the hill behind her, scrabbling over rocks, and when he reached the grassier plateau at the top he paused to catch his breath. "Where are you going? You have to come and take cover with the rest of us, anything could happen!"

"No, I need to get away," Leaf muttered. "You should go back. Look after Seeker and the others. Stay away from me."

Dasher looked up at the dark sky and shuddered.

"What are you talking about?" he said. "You're our Dragon Speaker, we need you!"

"This is all my fault, Dasher. You have to go. Your mother needs you. They all do."

Dasher hesitated. Then he ran across the grass to her side, and wound around her legs, pressing his face to hers.

"All right," he said. "I'll be with the others. But come back soon. We'll figure this out, together."

"All right," Leaf said, her voice coming out flat and tired. She watched him scamper away, her heart hurting.

He'll be back. He'll come and find me, and I can't let him. The best thing I can do for them now is just . . . go.

She walked on, first crossing the plateau, and then back down the other side of the hill. She wandered aimlessly, turning this way and that, circling a tree and then stepping out onto a mossy rock that stuck out of the side of the slope.

And then, as she was standing on that rock and looking out over the kingdom, a burst of light emerged from one side of the black disc that made her eyes sting. The light grew, the colors bright and the shadows claw-sharp in its strange dawn. Finally, the black disc rolled away.

The sun was back. The kingdom had been spared.

Leaf's heart broke.

"Great Dragon," she said, "I understand. I'm doing the right thing, walking away from the red pandas. Everything looks the same . . . but everything has changed."

She took out her stone, holding it up to glint in the strange light. Its green surface shimmered, like a reflection of the trees . . .

And turned black.

Leaf gasped and dropped the stone. It landed in the moss with a thump, and lay there looking like a tiny Dark Sun. Leaf backed away from it, swallowing a cry of anguish.

"I understand," she said again.

She paused, digging her claws into the moss and trying to gather herself, trying not to fall apart.

She did understand.

She would never forget the cries of the red pandas. She'd done everything she could to help them, and it hadn't been enough. She would never forgive herself for that, and it didn't surprise her that the Great Dragon couldn't either.

The Great Dragon knew all along. The Dark Sun was my warning, and it came true because I led them into danger. And now the stone has rejected me too.

She stepped forward and picked up the stone. As she did, the green color came back, just like the Dark Sun passing and the sun coming out in the kingdom. But this dawn wasn't for her. The stone had made that clear.

"But I tried *so hard*. . . ."

She choked on her words. Everything had gone so wrong, and she couldn't even say when it had happened. Perhaps the three Dragon Speakers shouldn't have split up. Perhaps something broke when they parted from each other. That had been her idea, too, so it made sense that it had been a bad one.

"I'll leave it here," she said, laying the stone down on top of a flat rock, where it glinted and shone in the strange light. "You'll make sure it finds its way to the right creature—to a good Dragon Speaker."

She wanted to feel like a weight had lifted from her, but she didn't. She thought it would be a long time before she could feel anything but guilt and failure.

She fixed her gaze on the distant horizon, not the Prosperhill or the White Spine Mountains, but the place where the sun rose in the mornings, where the river flowed into . . . well, where? What was over there, beyond the kingdom as they knew it? Perhaps, if she was very lucky, she might find a place where no one knew her, maybe where no creature had even heard of the Great Dragon or the Dragon Speakers.

She suddenly thought about her mother, Orchid. She had vanished, when the triplets were born, to keep them safe. She had given up her life, her family, for the good of the kingdom.

Leaf would do the same. She would become a panda in exile, follow the river until it ran dry or she couldn't walk anymore.

Leaf looked back toward the red pandas one last time. Dasher would understand, in the end. Things would be better, when she was gone, and then he'd understand.

She turned her face to the sky, and walked toward the sunrise.

CHAPTER TWENTY

WHEN THE DARKNESS HAD come, Ghost had looked up at the Dark Sun in dismay . . . but also, with a strange sense of enchantment. He continued to travel up into the mountains, watching the shimmering circle of light around the black sun, and looking at the stars. It was so odd, and so beautiful. And then, as suddenly as it had fallen, the darkness lifted, and he found himself standing on a snowy slope that blazed with the light of sunrise, even though it was the middle of the day. He felt his white fur warming under the sun.

I'm home.

There was a peace to coming back to the White Spine Mountains, even now. The sight of the lonely pine trees twisting between the rocks, the feel of snow crunching underneath his paws. It wouldn't be an easy life, but when had it ever been?

I just wish . . .

He shook himself, and put one paw in front of the other. There was no point in wishing, not now. He may never see Leaf or Rain again. He probably wouldn't have the chance to say he was sorry.

They had turned on him, both of them, with an ease that still made his skin crawl. But the more distance he put between them, the worse he felt about his own reaction. He could have been more careful, tried harder to fit in with the other pandas. He longed to apologize to them both, but whenever he considered turning back and facing them again, he just couldn't find the words.

In any case, he wasn't sure what awful thing had happened to cause the Dark Sun, but perhaps Leaf's doubts were right, and none of them were cut out to be Dragon Speakers.

He didn't want to believe it. He didn't want to forget the feeling of standing in the presence of the Great Dragon, or everything they had gone through to find each other. But what could he do, if neither of them were willing to listen to him?

He climbed the snowy slopes, leaving blue-black paw prints behind him in the snow as the shadows seemed to pool in them like water. He found a stony path that was sheltered enough for grass to grow thick and green between the rocks, and thought about the blue sheep. If they came to him again, he would tell them about this place. They wouldn't, but he would remember anyway. Just in case.

The one thing he knew for certain was that he would find his other family, his first family, up here in the mountains. Snowstorm and Frost were still living here, and Shiver must have known that if they got separated this would be the place to find him. She probably would have gone back to Winter's old den—at least, that's where *he* would go, so that's where he was heading. And when they were reunited, and he had his stone once more . . .

Then what? Do I just go on as I've been? Do I try to be the Dragon Speaker for the mountains, even if they don't want me?

He turned the possibilities over in his mind as he walked, over ridges and plateaus and rocky scrambles that seemed more and more familiar with every step. If Brisk and Sleet left him alone, he might have some chance of persuading the other mountain creatures that he wasn't dangerous. But really, how likely was it that they would leave him alone for very long? They would be back eventually.

Perhaps he should take the stone to the Dragon Mountain. There, he was sure, either the Dragon would have some guidance for him or perhaps he could give it away to another keeper, one who could use it?

By the time he was close to the den, the light had softened and the sun blazed less fiercely, and it had also started snowing. Ghost chuckled to himself as he passed a small clump of trees where the Snow Cat had led him to prey—things really were going back to normal. Here he was, climbing over the rocks in the snow, the cliff that contained his mother's den looming just over the next plateau.

He looked for the mouth of the den, through the swirling flakes, and he saw the faint patch of darker stone against the side of the cliff, and then he saw the leopard shape sitting just outside it.

Shiver!

He clambered up over the last rock and took a few steps forward, and then realized that the leopard shape was actually *two*, both bigger than Shiver. It was Snowstorm and Frost! Perhaps Shiver was inside, or maybe he'd got there first. If so, his siblings were in for a big surprise. . . .

The leopards turned to look at him, and he skidded to a stop. That wasn't Snowstorm, or Frost. A flurry of snow passed between them, obscuring the other leopards' faces, but they'd already seen him. Through the swirling white he could see that they were standing, and then starting to run toward him.

It was Brisk and Sleet.

Ghost stood his ground, a furious roar building in his chest. Would he never be rid of them, not even for a moment?

And where is Shiver?

At the last minute he threw himself aside and rolled out of the way. The two leopards skidded past him, and Brisk slid right over the edge of the rocks and caught himself with his front claws.

"Come on, then!" Ghost roared as he backed away, growling and snapping at the air, but all the time moving to the higher, flatter ground. He had to get off the steep slopes, or he wouldn't stand a chance. "Let's be done with this, once and for all!"

Sleet came around and charged him again, and this time he dug his claws in and hunkered down just as she was about to strike him, using his strong shoulders and her own momentum to heave her up and over his back. She sprawled in the snow and he hurried farther up the slope.

"It's over, freak," said Brisk, shaking himself as he clambered back up onto the slope below. "You're going to die here, all alone. Your precious siblings will find you frozen into the ice."

"*Why?*" Ghost snarled. "What could you possibly gain? Why would you seek me out?"

Sleet rolled onto her paws and started after him, closing the gap between them alarmingly fast.

"Are you *jealous* of me being a Dragon Speaker?" Ghost improvised. "That has to be it—I'm no threat to you, I can't jump or run or hunt like you, you established that every day when we were cubs!" This made Brisk and Sleet snicker to each other, which was fine by Ghost. He was buying himself time, backing away step by step. They were slinking after him, keeping pace, but that wasn't so important—he was nearly at the top of the slope now, and up there he knew there was a flatter snow plain, long stone paths, and the plateau of the Endless Maw. He was stronger than them. He just had to get them onto ground where they wouldn't have even *more* of an advantage . . .

"Why do you hate me so much you'd follow me all over the kingdom?" he demanded.

Brisk and Sleet actually stopped walking, and looked at each other. A prickling started under Ghost's fur. He'd only asked to buy more time, but now he had a very bad feeling about that look.

"Well, since you're not going to live to see the next dawn," Sleet sneered, "maybe it'll be comforting to know that you're not the only one with brand-new friends."

"And when we get rid of you, we're helping them, too. We keep you out of our territory, *and* out of Brawnshanks's golden hair," Brisk chuckled. "A perfect arrangement. His friend Crookedclaw gave us a lot of really good ideas."

Brawnshanks...

Ghost gazed over Brisk's and Sleet's heads, down the mountain slopes. His stomach felt as if it had turned to a block of ice, heavy and cold in his belly. How much had the monkeys been behind, all this time? He had barely glimpsed one of the blue-faced menaces since Dusk had been exposed as a traitor. Leaf had mentioned them, but he hadn't been listening. He'd run the length of the kingdom, chasing these two leopards . . . and all the time, had he really just been chasing Brawnshanks's shadow?

The snow leopards pounced. Ghost scrambled backward, cursing himself for letting them distract him, and managed to catch Sleet with a swipe across the face, but it was desperate and sloppy. Brisk was on him in a blink, teeth in the fur of his back leg, trying to drag him onto his belly. He braced himself and kicked out with his other leg, catching Brisk on the top of the head. Brisk yowled and let go, and Ghost was free to turn and sprint as hard as he could for the flat ground at the top of the cliff.

But he couldn't outrun them. He made it to the top, only slipping backward in the snow once, but as soon as he stumbled over the lip of the cliff and onto the plain he felt one of them land on his back. It was Sleet, and his teeth were in the back of his neck. He screamed with pain as he felt them clamp on tight.

This is real. He's trying to kill me.

His neck was too strong and too thick for the young leopard to press down and suffocate him like a piece of prey, and that probably saved his life. He flopped over on his side, putting everything he had into falling hard and rolling so that Sleet was thrown down underneath him. He managed to tear his teeth from his neck, though the pain was unbearable. He saw red, the snow in the air seeming to throb along with the pulse of his heart as he scrambled to his paws and then brought them down hard on his exposed chest with a furious, desperate roar. Sleet let out a wheezing cry as the breath was pushed out of him.

Ghost disengaged and stumbled away just in time to avoid a second bite from Brisk. He tried to run, but he couldn't see or walk straight; his paws got in his way and he tumbled into the snow. He tried to get up again. Brisk was advancing slowly, a high-pitched excited growl coming from her chest at the sight of Ghost's struggles. Ghost shook his head, backed up against a snowdrift, and bared his teeth. Brisk hesitated, seeing the danger. She tried to feint to the left and then lunge right, but Ghost saw the flick of her ears and dodged out of the way. They circled each other as Sleet pulled himself up from the snow, panting and spluttering.

Ghost lunged first, and managed to close his powerful jaws around Brisk's coat, and he came away with a mouthful of fur. Brisk yowled, and Ghost spat the fur into the snow, and saw that he had wounded her, but shallowly. Brisk turned on him, blood dribbling through her white fur, and brought both paws down, claws out, to rake across Ghost's back. Another burst of red crossed Ghost's vision. Brisk's tail passed before his eyes and Ghost bit down hard on it and tugged, dragging Brisk off balance and onto her side. But before Ghost could go for Brisk's throat, Sleet was there again, his eyes wild. He threw Ghost onto his back, and would have bitten into his belly if Ghost hadn't got his paws up in time—he fell on his long, hard claws and they dug into his shoulder. He snapped and yowled down at him, not quite able to reach, and he tried to push him away, but every pulse of his heart made the world swim and stutter. . . .

I can't do this, he thought. *I can't fight them both alone! Great Dragon, help me, please!*

With a huge grunt of effort he threw Sleet off him and got to his feet. The snow was coming thicker and thicker now, and a whirling flurry suddenly passed in front of Ghost's face, obscuring the leopards for a moment even though they were just a bear-length away. He took the opportunity to limp backward, to try to run, and when he looked around he saw something else moving in the snow.

Shiver? he thought. *Please, let it be . . .*

But it was too big to be Shiver. It was too big to be a leopard at all—a wide face on a muscular body. It crouched, gracefully, as if it was about to pounce, and then it turned and bounded away from him, its thin striped tail swishing as it vanished into the snow.

Shadowhunter?

Memories flooded into Ghost's mind, even as he stumbled after the tiger, leaving the two leopards growling into the snow flurries. Shadowhunter the tiger, who had saved him from the monkeys in the Broken Forest, who'd been sent by the Great Dragon to protect the Dragon Speakers . . . who had carried Dusk Deepwood over the edge of the chasm at the heart of the Dragon Mountain.

He couldn't be alive, but here he was—a vision, sent by the Dragon one last time?

There was too much pain in his back and freezing snow in his eyes for Ghost to think clearly, but Shadowhunter's striped tail was still faintly visible, running in front of him, and so Ghost followed.

"There he is!" he heard Brisk shout. The snow must have cleared for a moment. He kept on running. Shadowhunter would take him to safety.

Just when he thought he couldn't go any farther, he saw something dark up ahead, and the snow cleared.

Ghost skidded to a halt, gasping for breath, his heart sinking.

The Endless Maw lay in front of him, the great chasm in the ground, with the single column in the center and its icy, slippery rock walls. It was a dead end, at least for him.

Was this the Great Dragon's way of telling him his time was over? That he could choose how he would die—torn to shreds by Brisk and Sleet, or plummeting to the bottom?

"Well, well," said Sleet. He was sneaking up toward him, Brisk limping on his heels. "What are you going to do now?"

"It's time you joined your mother at the bottom of the Maw," Brisk chuckled.

Despite himself, Ghost almost felt like smiling. Brisk was saying that to be cruel, but perhaps she was right. Perhaps this was justice, somehow. . . . .

Then a roar echoed between the peaks of the White Spine Mountains. Ghost, Brisk, and Sleet all startled, and Ghost's heart began to pound again.

That wasn't a leopard sound, and it wasn't the bark of a panda, either. That was the roar of a *bigger* cat, and the leopards had heard it too, which meant . . .

He turned just in time to see the tiger spring from the rock column in the middle of the Maw, crossing the chasm in an easy-looking bound. She landed beside him in a burst of snow and roared again, her huge jaws opening wide, hot breath rippling through the air toward Brisk and Sleet. They shuddered, their ears pinning back to their heads in fright.

"Back off," she snarled, stalking in front of Ghost, her thin tail lashing the air.

Ghost realized that she wasn't a fully-grown tiger—at least, not as big as Shadowhunter had been—but she was still bigger than the young snow leopards, and when she took a single step toward them they almost fell over each other in desperation to get away from her.

"Ghost, follow me," she said, and turned back to the Maw.

Ghost's heart sank, and he opened his mouth to tell her to stop, to say he couldn't make that jump—but then she vanished, not across to the column, but down, below the lip of the cliff. He edged after her and looked over. There was a ledge there, a few bear-lengths down. She landed gracefully and disappeared, apparently right into the rock.

Ghost swallowed. It was an easy enough drop for a tiger, harder for a panda with no tail to balance with and wounds that were starting to close simply because the blood was freezing around them. But what choice did he have?

He slipped over the edge. He heard Brisk yowl "What in the White Spine . . . ?" as he slid down the icy rock, his claws dragging on the stone to try to control his fall. His hindquarters hit the snowy ledge and he scrambled for a grip on the rock, flattening himself against it. Then he looked up, and saw the face of the young tiger staring out of the cliff wall.

"Follow me! Quick, so they don't know where we've gone!" she hissed.

Ghost got to his paws and limped at the wall, and realized that what he was seeing was a sort of cave entrance—a hole in the rock just large enough for him to wiggle through, but not dark inside. From above, the cave would be impossible to see. Brisk and Sleet would probably think he'd fallen to his death, and Ghost knew they wouldn't be brave enough to climb down and check.

He was free.

The tiger turned around, with a little difficulty, in the small space, and started to walk away from Ghost. He realized that this cave was a tunnel, gently sloping down, and not enclosed on all sides—more breaks in the cliff wall like the one they'd climbed in through let in the light, and let him see out into the Endless Maw.

"Keep up," the tiger said. "I don't want to be in here too long."

It was a surreal feeling to be *walking* down the Maw. The floor of the tunnel was icy, and he slipped more than once, but never slid down too far before there was a snowdrift or a pile of rocks to catch him. Icicles hung in the gaps in the cliff wall, and he found himself staring out every time he passed one. He saw less snow as they descended, and more ice, and then he started to see a few spiky plant leaves, and the snowcapped tops of trees.

It was beautiful. If he hadn't been aching all over, he would have thought it was all a strange dream. But his wounds never let him forget they were there, and after a little while his paws ached from walking on ice for so long. By the time they were approaching the bottom of the Maw he felt as if he could lie down in the snow and sleep for days, however terrible an idea that would be.

He squeezed over a tree root that had grown through the middle of the tunnel, and found himself standing in snow once more. The bottom of the Maw was a thin valley, with a few tall fir trees, growing despite the snow and the lack of light. Their branches hung with glittering icicles, and sparkling frost-covered grasses crept through the cracks in the rocks. Ghost stared, his heart swelling a little. He'd only ever thought of the Maw as a place of death, but even down here in the deep shadows, life had found a way to carry on.

Then his gaze fell on a shape in the snow, and he gasped and stumbled over to it.

It was the skeleton of a leopard.

"Mother," he whispered.

He was sure it was Winter. Her bones lay in a strangely natural-looking pose, almost as if she had simply fallen asleep in the snow. Tiny, delicate white flowers were growing in the sheltered places she'd made, poking their fragile petals between her ribs and around the back of her skull.

He'd yearned to see her again, to tell her that he was sorry, but he had never imagined this. She looked . . . peaceful.

"Thank you," he said, and gently touched his muzzle between her eye sockets.

I owe her so much. She believed in me, right to the end. And she wouldn't want me to give up because of Brisk and Sleet, or because of Brawnshanks. She would want me to fight on.

He looked up and saw the tiger sitting in the snow nearby, watching him carefully.

"I'm here to help you fight," she said, as if she'd heard his thoughts.

"What's your name?" Ghost asked.

"Nightwalker," said the tiger. "Shadowhunter was my uncle. When he died, I was called—the Great Dragon told me that all was not well, that the Dragon Speakers would need their Watcher, so I came. It seems I was just in time."

"I hope so," said Ghost. "I think the monkeys have done something awful, while we were all chasing shadows. I was accused of killing another panda, and I gave my Speaker stone to my littermate Shiver, and I haven't found her yet—and I think both my sisters are in terrible trouble."

Nightwalker stood up, and shook out her mane. "Then we'd better get going," she said. "It sounds like you and I have a lot of work to do."

CHAPTER TWENTY-ONE

"No sign at all?" Crookedclaw said. She didn't seem angry, but thoughtful. She scratched her chin as she sat on a log in the secret meeting place behind the rotting branches, looking around at her gathered spies. They all shook their heads. "Interesting," said Crookedclaw. "And the pangolins *definitely* said that before the Great Dragon, they were seen in the kingdom? The light and dark dragons? They weren't invisible?"

"That's what they told me," said Strikepaw. "They didn't seem to know why there's no trace of them—or why there are now three."

"Interesting," Crookedclaw said again. She fell silent for a moment, and all her spies stayed obediently quiet while she considered.

Nimbletail's ears were burning as she sat and waited, fully

aware that she was one monkey alone in a group that would kill her if they knew what she knew. But she was almost used to the discomfort now, after a few days of constantly being terrified that any minute she'd be exposed and Crookedclaw would have her thrown into the lava, with Quicktail and the rest of her band. She knew she was probably living on borrowed time.

"No one can hide from me forever," said Crookedclaw. "Three dragons left that cave, and if they exist, they can be found and destroyed. You will all play a part in this, I guarantee. When I send you to search the kingdom, you listen to everything, consider all possibilities, and we will find them."

The spies, including Nimbletail, nodded silently. Nimbletail had noticed that even when they were all together, they didn't whoop and cheer like the Strong Arms. They were all smart, thoughtful monkeys—well, apart from Briskhand, who made up for it with determination and cruelty—and that made them far more dangerous.

"In the meantime, I have better news from the north. We may have three Dragons, but we only have two Speakers to worry about. Ghost will be dead by now. Our allies have done good work. He is isolated, demoralized, without his stone— which we didn't even steal, he threw it away himself," she added, with a horrible chuckle. "The leopards have their orders to finish him off, and we can turn our attention south. Rain is our next target. Our ally there is already in place, but I need one of you to go to the Prosperhill to observe their progress."

Nimbletail's hair stood on end. She saw Briskhand begin to raise his hand, and thrust hers into the air, with a bit too much enthusiasm.

"I'll go," she said.

Briskhand gave her an angry scowl.

"So eager," said Crookedclaw. "Why?"

"I know the territory," Nimbletail answered. She took a deep breath. "It just makes sense—I was one of the monkeys chosen to guard Rain and her mother, when they were in the prison pit. I got to know her a bit, from all that watching. She's stubborn. And her experience with Dusk means if she senses something wrong, she'll worry at it like a fox with a bone until she figures out what's happening. I think I know some ways we can keep her distracted."

None of which was a lie, or if it was, it was so close to the truth you couldn't see light between them.

At least, she hoped so.

Crookedclaw regarded her for a moment longer, then nodded and waved a long-fingered hand. "Good. You should go. Just watch her, for the moment, and be prepared to report in to me."

"I will," said Nimbletail. She gave an awkward bow and slipped out of the den.

She walked into the forest, heading back toward her band's tree. She felt a spring in her step, for the first time in a long time. She would be away from Crookedclaw, able to tell Rain that she was in danger, and all about what had happened to the Dragons. . . .

"Nimbletail," said Crookedclaw's voice behind her. Nimbletail froze, then turned slowly to see Crookedclaw emerging from behind a brown fern. "A word."

"Of course," she said brightly, but not too brightly, she hoped.

"I just wanted to say that you're doing a good job," Crookedclaw told her. "But if you do anything to mess this up, Quicktail will die a slow death. Is that understood?"

Nimbletail swallowed, and then, although it almost physically hurt her, she forced herself to laugh as if she thought Crookedclaw's threat had been a joke. "Noted," she said. "I won't mess it up, I promise."

Crookedclaw smiled back, but there was no warmth in it. "Get going, then," she said, and walked back toward the hidden den.

She's sort of right, Nimbletail thought, watching her go. *Quicktail is relying on me—and so's the rest of the Bamboo Kingdom! I can't mess this up. . . .*

Nimbletail arrived in the Southern Forest as the sun was setting that day, but she didn't talk to Rain right away. Crookedclaw might be on the side of destruction and chaos, but she was right about some things. It was better to watch and listen than charge in and give away your plan. So she hid in the high tops of the trees, where even the pandas who liked to climb couldn't get to, and watched the Prosperhill as the pandas went about their business.

Immediately she noticed that Rain was almost never all

alone. Half the time she was talking to creatures who needed a Dragon Speaker, and when she wasn't doing that she was walking with her mother, or tending to the Prosperhill pandas, or swimming with her friend Lychee. Even when she slept, she was often cuddled up pretty close to Lychee or Peony.

Nimbletail tried to watch the petitioners carefully. She suspected at least one of them was a spy for Crookedclaw too. She had said someone in the south was an ally, but Nimbletail couldn't guess which creature it was.

Finally, Nimbletail got her chance. The Feast of Sun Fall was coming up, and all the pandas were gathering bamboo, including Rain. She was climbing a tall bamboo trunk, one of the mighty black ones that could be mistaken for trees, to get to the tender leaves at the top. Nimbletail followed, springing quietly from trunk to trunk, and thinking of the Second Feat. The stalactites had been easier to grip, but at least she could see where she was going.

Rain bit off an offshoot of the cane with a loud snap, and dropped it to the ground, and Nimbletail chose that moment to make the leap to the trunk right beside Rain's.

Rain yelped and slipped down to the next section of the bamboo trunk, her claws leaving grooves in the bark.

"What are you doing?" she snapped. "What do you want?"

"Shh!" Nimbletail slid down too, panic gripping her—there were pandas down on the ground, and if they looked up and saw her talking to Rain and then it got back to Crookedclaw somehow . . .

"Did Brawnshanks send you?" Rain growled. "Is he—"

"Shh!" In desperation, Nimbletail jumped to the same trunk Rain was holding on to, and then clamped her hands over Rain's jaws, holding them shut. "Shh, please!"

"Mmmf! Mmhmm!" Rain wriggled and tried to get Nimbletail's hands into her mouth to bite them, but Nimbletail climbed onto her back and looped her arm around Rain's muzzle.

What am I doing?! she thought, as the bamboo bent and swayed underneath them.

"Please just listen!" she hissed. "I'm here to help you, you're in terrible danger!"

Rain stopped wriggling, though Nimbletail could feel the tension in her shoulders where her paws were resting.

"Please, Speaker, be quiet! If anyone knows I'm here it'll be bad, for both of us. If they know I'm helping you, they'll kill me *and* my sister. So . . . I'm going to let go now."

"Mm," said Rain shortly.

Gingerly, Nimbletail took her hands away, and then sprang to the neighboring bamboo trunk just in case. Rain glared at her.

"I know you," she snarled—though to Nimbletail's relief, she did keep her voice low. "You were there when Brawnshanks kept me and my mother prisoner! Tell me why I shouldn't scream and bring half the Prosperhill over here to catch you?"

"Yes, I was there," Nimbletail said. "But! I was the monkey

that came and led the other guards away, so you could escape! Shiver asked me to do it. I'm not on Brawnshanks's side," she whispered. "He's done something terrible, and he's going to do worse if we don't stop him."

Rain seemed to think about this for a moment, and then shifted position on the bamboo trunk, digging her back claws in to a rough patch in the bark. Nimbletail realized she was making sure she could hold on for longer, and her spirits rose. Rain was ready to listen.

"Tell me everything," she said. "And then I'll decide if I believe you."

Nimbletail took a deep breath.

"Well, for a start . . . something's happened to the Great Dragon," she said.

Rain listened, and didn't interrupt, as Nimbletail spilled out everything she knew, starting with the capture of the pangolins, the attempt to split the Dragon into two, the strange third dragon and the monkey's failed attempts to hunt them down, and then Crookedclaw's plans for the Dragon Speakers. Rain's eyes grew wide as Nimbletail talked about the leopards who'd ruined Ghost's chances at being a good Speaker.

"Brisk and Sleet," she muttered. "They . . . they really were here?"

"I think so," said Nimbletail. "And . . . and Crookedclaw says that by now they will have ambushed Ghost in the mountains, and . . . killed him."

Rain slid a little way down the bamboo, caught herself, and

leaned her forehead on the black bark, her breath coming in ragged gasps.

"Oh, Great Dragon . . . what have I done?" Rain said. "He didn't kill Pebble, did he? I can't believe I thought that. . . . I was just so angry . . . oh, Ghost . . ." She took a deep, shaky breath. "And you think I'm next. That this monkey plot is coming here, to destroy me?"

Nimbletail nodded. "But for now, they've sent me. And I'm not going to do anything to hurt you," she said. "I'm sorry about your brother. But even if it's just you and me, we can still do something. I can be your spy in the monkey camp, tell you everything Crookedclaw asks me to do, and we can figure out how to help the Dragon."

She paused, looking out over the Bamboo Kingdom, foolishly half hoping she would catch a glimpse of the light or dark or shining dragons moving among the trees. There was nothing . . . but that was all right.

"There's always something you can do," she said. "I learned that from the pangolins. I couldn't save them all, I was too late to stop them being captured—but I saved *some* of them, and after the darkness, the sun rose. That means there's still hope."

Rain sniffed, looked up and met Nimbletail's eyes. "That's right. Even if Ghost is gone . . . even if the *Dragon* is gone . . . I'm not going to let Brawnshanks win. We'll stop him. Together."

EPILOGUE

Rain was sitting alone after the Feast of Sun Fall, watching a gust of wind blowing a swirl of leaves round and round in circles, when Lychee came up to her. He sat nearby, not so close they were touching, but close enough that she knew he was there. He didn't say anything.

She liked an awful lot of things about Lychee, but the way he always seemed to know when she wanted to talk and when she didn't was one of her favorites. She shifted a little closer to him so that her shoulder brushed his.

"Can I help?" he asked.

Rain sighed.

I accused my brother of killing my best friend, my mystical guide has been split in three, and the monkeys are out to get me.

She turned and smiled at him. "No," she said. "I don't think you can. Not yet."

"I'm sorry," he said. "I miss Pebble too. I wish . . . I wish you'd had a chance to properly make up. He seemed like a really good panda."

Rain nodded sadly. She opened her mouth to say something, maybe *I need to find out who really killed him* or *we made a terrible mistake* . . . but then she closed it again.

She liked Lychee. She *really* liked him. And that was all the more reason to keep him out of this, at least for now.

"Will you . . . will you be here?" she said. "When I'm ready to ask for your help?"

"Always," said Lychee. His voice was light, but his eyes looked serious, and Rain's heart skipped a beat.

Is this what it's like to have a mate? she wondered. Of course, nothing had been said, nothing official . . . but she knew he felt the same.

"I'll be by the river, if anyone needs me," she said, getting to her paws. Lychee simply nodded, and watched her walk away down the panda path.

Down by the water's edge, Rain took out her Dragon Speaker stone and held it in her paw, rolling it back and forth, feeling the smooth, odd-shaped edges where it should have fit perfectly into a sphere with the other two stones.

We were the triplets, she thought. *We were always three, even when we didn't know that. Can we really be only two now? Can Ghost really be gone?*

She knew she shouldn't have rejected him. She *knew* she was wrong not to stand up for him—from the moment the words left her mouth, it had been gnawing at her. And it hurt more, that she knew and still let it happen, than if she'd really thought he was at fault. She'd just been so blinded with grief, she'd hardly understood what she was saying. . . .

That's no excuse, she told herself.

And now, Leaf . . . was she dead, too? Was she in hiding? Word had come from the north that the red pandas were frantic, that she had vanished right as the Dark Sun hit its peak.

"Great Dragon . . . I know you're not there," she said, pressing her stone to her heart. "But if anyone can figure this out, it's Leaf! She was always the best one, and now she's missing, and it's just me, and . . . and I don't know if I can do it alone."

She sighed, and opened her paw.

The blue stone shimmered, and changed. At first it seemed like looking into a deep clear pool of water, with dancing shattered rainbow lights refracting on the bottom. Then it turned completely clear, except . . . something was still moving within it . . .

Then the blue came back, solid as ever.

Rain smiled to herself, and folded the stone close to her chest once more.

She didn't understand everything that was happening— but she would. It was time to be a real Dragon Speaker, to find Pebble's killer and stand up for the Bamboo Kingdom. It wouldn't be easy. But no matter what, she knew she wouldn't be alone.

ship
RY

Jeffersonville Township
PUBLIC LIBRARY

jefflibrary.org